GERARD SIGGINS

RUGBY REDZONE

SPORTS ACADEMY

THE O'BRIEN PRESS
DUBLIN

First published 2019 by
The O'Brien Press Ltd,
12 Terenure Road East, Rathgar,
Dublin 6, D06 HD27 Ireland.

Tel: +353 1 4923333; Fax: +353 1 4922777
E-mail: books@obrien.ie
Website: www.obrien.ie

The O'Brien Press is a member of Publishing Ireland
ISBN: 978-1-78849-141-9
Text © copyright Gerard Siggins 2019

1 3 5 7 8 6 4 2

19 21 23 22 20

Printed and bound by CPI Group (UK) Ltd, Croydon, CR0 4YY.
The paper in this book is produced using pulp from managed forests.

Published in

DUBLIN

UNESCO
City of Literature

DEDICATION

To Maureen, Fergus and all who made the journey with us; great days.

Acknowledgements

Thanks as ever to Martha, Jack, Lucy and Billy for the time, space and encouragement.

Thanks to Mam and Dad for all the support.

And thanks to my editor, Helen Carr, who always makes these books so much better.

CHAPTER 1

Whenever Kim couldn't sleep she went for a long walk. Living on a submarine, that wasn't as easy as it might sound, but Kim had a good imagination.

Creeping past her roommate's bed, Kim grinned as she listened to the snorts and whistles made by Jess – and made a mental note to record them and play them back to her some morning. As silently as possible, she let herself out of the room and headed down the corridor.

The submarine, which was disguised as a small island, purred gently as it travelled through the ocean. Kim didn't have much of an idea where they were, preferring to leave all that to the captain, and Luce, who ran the Atlantis Academy.

Kim had been selected for the sports programme some months before, despite being a very ordinary performer on her primary school rugby team. The rest of the kids were just as bad at their favourite sports, but all shared a determination and willingness to get better.

So far, the students had all shown huge improvements, especially in football where they had a brilliant, eccentric coach to inspire them, and had helped Atlantis win a crucial match deep in the jungles of South America.

Kim wandered through the school till she found her favourite room, the sporting simulator. It was here they could practise by taking penalties against the best goal-keeper in the world, or even play a game of tennis against a hologram of a legendary player. Kim liked to go for walks but found it boring doing so around the gloomy corridors, so she came up with a brilliant plan – she slowed a running machine down to a gentle pace and adjusted the video pictures that bathed the room so it showed a golf course, or the route of every Olympic marathon race.

'I think I'd like to see what Beijing looks like at this time of year,' she chuckled to herself, as she hopped onto the walking machine.

It wasn't easy to find space to keep to yourself on a submarine, and Kim enjoyed it whenever she could get it, even if it was at the cost of sleep. She always loved walks in the countryside to relax back at home, but this was a different type of exercise, and she found it interesting to see how people lived in other countries. She hadn't travelled much before her Atlantis adventure had begun and even since they had very little taste of the places they had visited. She hoped that would change.

She was really getting into her walk, even waving at some of the people she passed on her journey around the Chinese city, when a knock came to the door. In walked Kelly, the talent scout who had invited Kim to Atlantis Academy.

'Hi, Kim,' she said, with a big grin. 'Great to see you, even at this ridiculous hour.'

'Wow, hi, Kelly,' frowned Kim as she checked her watch and saw that it was 3am.

'Are you finding it hard to sleep too? This is my first night on board and I can't get used to the movement.'

'It's not bad after a while, I just can't sleep when Jess is snoring,' Kim said, smiling.

Kelly laughed. 'Great to see you using the machines so creatively, I was watching you on the monitors up in the control room.'

'Really? They can see us up there?' replied Kim, blushing. 'Waving at the crowds and all?'

'Well, yes, I suppose they have to keep tabs on where

everyone is.'

'So, when did you arrive?' asked Kim, changing the subject.

'Last night, about ten o'clock,' said Kelly. 'I flew to Boston and then took a little boat out into the Atlantic with one of Kalvin's friends. The island came to the surface and I hopped on board. I wasn't surprised there wasn't a welcoming party. It was verrrrrrry cold.'

'And why did you come?'

'Oh, sorry, have they not explained? We're on the second phase of your training now. You're going to the Rugby World Cup.'

CHAPTER 2

Back in her bed, Kim tried hard to sleep but Kelly's arrival had just given her brain more to buzz about. She had really enjoyed learning and playing football, but rugby was the sport that she loved the most.

Her dad had been a good player back home, but too many injuries forced him to give it up before she was born. She loved going to watch games with him and meeting his old friends, but one day he got sick and soon afterwards stopped going. Life got harder for Kim and her little brother; their mum was hardly around after she had to take up a second job.

Then one day Kim saw a poster in school asking for girls to join a new rugby team so she put her name down. She wasn't very good, but she knew all the laws and had loads of good ideas and tips which helped her friends. Her dad started coming along to watch their games, and even their training sessions.

'This is such a tonic for your father,' her mum confided in

her one day. 'Since he got sick he hasn't had much interest in anything, but your rugby has been a great boost to him.'

Kim couldn't wait to find out more about the World Cup so she could tell him on the next of the monthly video phone calls they were permitted. Although she hadn't even held a rugby ball since she arrived on Atlantis she knew that all the training and fitness work had made her a better player.

It felt like she had been asleep for five minutes when the alarm clock rang, and Jess sprang up out of her bed on the other side of the room.

'Good morning, Kimmy!' she called, sounding far more energetic and enthusiastic than Kim felt.

'Uhhhhhhmmmnggg,' she grunted in reply.

Kim lifted her legs off the bed slowly, one by one. She buried her face in her hands and tried to rub the sleep out of her eyes. She loved Jess – everyone did – but she could be a little giddy just when you didn't want her to be.

'You look wretched, Kimmy,' said Jess.

'I didn't sleep well,' she replied, 'I even went for a walk to try to tire myself out but that was interrupted.' She explained about Kelly and her news.

'Wow! A World Cup? That will be awesome, I wonder when we're going to learn how to play this sport though…'

Kim laughed, and then went white. 'Oh no… of course… I'm the only one who's ever played rugby before!'

That wasn't quite true, she discovered over breakfast with the rest of her classmates.

'I joined a club last winter,' explained Craig. 'We had a really horrible coach though, so I gave up after three or four sessions. I really enjoyed playing though and love watching it on TV.'

Craig had joined the Academy as a tennis player, but like all the kids he was expected to throw himself into every sport that was offered to him. Jess was mainly an athlete, while Ajit had been picked because of one flash of magic he'd shown when using his cricket skills in a hurling match. Joe had been the worst footballer on his club team, but he loved the sport and was willing to work hard to improve and the scout valued that most of all. He was recruited by Atlantis Academy and captained the football team to victory in that high-stakes match in Brazil.

'Yeah, the Six Nations is always great to watch,' agreed Joe. 'But it sometimes looks very rough…'

Joe's comment was interrupted by the arrival of Kelly, who asked could she join them.

'Let me guess, Joe,' she smiled. 'You're not talking about the table tennis tournament this morning?'

Joe grinned back at her. 'Ah no, I wouldn't mind playing rugby at all,' he said. 'It's just some of those forwards are HUGE, and when they run into you it must hurt a lot.'

'Well, yes, the adult game can be very physical, but when you're playing against people your own size it's a lot less harmful. But we'll train you all to do the right things and how to avoid damaging yourself or your opponent.'

'Tell us more about this World Cup,' asked Jess.

'Well…' Kelly started, 'I'm not sure how much I can say yet. But it's a special World Cup for kids that will be run alongside the main one in Japan. You'll be meeting lots of kids from all over the world, representing countries, schools, clubs – and independent island academies…'

'You mean besides us? Not that horrible one in Brazil?' asked Jess.

'No...' said Kelly. 'We're not the only school like this, you know. Although we are the only one that works like a submarine.'

'Japan!' said Craig. 'Wow, I've always wanted to go there...'

Ajit looked a bit concerned though. He stirred his smoothie and looked at Kelly.

'Hang on,' he started. 'Is it a five-a-side rugby competition? How does that work?'

'Ah... No,' replied Kelly. 'It will be Sevens... which means we're going to have to get you some new team-mates.'

CHAPTER 3

The five kids stared at Kelly.

'Really?' asked Kim. 'Where? Are we going back to Leap Island?'

Leap Island was where the five had first met on a cold and windy night some months before. They had each been selected at a couple of days' notice, plucked from their homes and brought to the west coast and from there out into a huge bay with 365 islands. Their guide explained that there was an island for every day of the year, but that an extra one – Leap Island – appeared briefly, once every four years on 29 February.

Kelly lifted her hand like a police officer at a roadblock.

'OK, I've probably told you more than I should have, but Luce will let you know later today. Now finish up here and let's get in the mood for some high-intensity physically-challenging table tennis!'

The coaches sat back and let the five organise their own table tennis competition, seeing it as a good way for the students to let off a bit of steam after a week under water. Craig was the best player, and the most ruthlessly competitive, and easily won his first three games, but Ajit had used his matches to practise a series of delicate drop shots. By the time they met in the final he kept glancing the ball into the corners just over the net which infuriated Craig and didn't let him play the big forehand smashes he enjoyed.

The other three were supporting Ajit, the underdog, which didn't make Craig any happier and he snapped at Joe when he was slow in tossing the ball back to him after it ran off the table.

'Uh, oh,' said Luce, who had just walked in. 'Maybe it's time to wind this down. You've all been cooped up indoors too long. We'll be getting some fresh air soon though. Come down to the canteen in ten minutes and I'll let you know what's happening over lunch.'

Luce left the room with Craig pleading to be allowed to finish the game. 'Come on Mr St Vincent,' he whined. 'I only need two points to win.'

'Nah, that's match abandoned,' said their West Indian

coach. 'Rain stop play. Call it a draw.'

Kim, Joe and Jess cheered as Ajit raised his bat above his head. Craig scowled and stormed off down the corridor.

He'd calmed down by the time his classmates joined him in the canteen, although that was probably because Luce was wagging her finger at him.

'All right kids, just pick up your lunch quickly and let's get down to business.'

The Sports Academy was careful to look after the nutritional needs of the students, so Maureen and Fleur, the old ladies in the kitchen, doled out their portions of fish and vegetables, with a yogurt for afters. The five sat down at a long table and were joined by Luce, Kelly and Deryck St Vincent.

'I think you may have got some unauthorised advance notice that we are going to the Rugby World Cup?' Luce started as she glanced across at Kelly, who was blushing.

'Well, it's a long way to Japan, and we have a lot of work to get you into shape, especially as I think only Kim and Craig have played the game before.'

Craig's eyes widened. 'Impressive, you've done your homework on me.'

Luce scowled and returned to her notes, explaining how, where and when the tournament would take place.

'It's a Sevens event, and we'll need a squad of ten, so we will obviously need to recruit some players to play alongside you. We are currently on course to link up with them in the next twenty-four hours. Has anyone any questions?'

Joe put up his hand. 'Where are we going to meet them? We're in the middle of the Atlantic the last time I looked.' There was a giant map in the control room and Joe often called down to track their progress around the oceans.

'Well… it's a special sort of place we're going,' said Luce. 'You're right, we're in the north Atlantic, just passing south of Iceland at the moment. I'll explain more about that when we're closer.

'The kids are all pupils at an academy that's similar to ours, although maybe not as sporty. The owner and Victor are great friends and have compared notes on the schools. They decided it would be good to link up for some projects and this was the first suitable one that came up.'

'And where will the kids stay?' asked Jess.

'Well… I'm afraid you're all going to have to tighten up a bit,' explained Luce. 'We're having the dorms adapted so you'll have to get used to bunk beds.'

'Ah no,' said Ajit. 'We're already crowded in our room.'

'It's just for a few weeks,' said Luce.

'*Weeeeeeks?*' wailed Craig.

Everyone laughed, and Craig even joined in.

'Yes Craig, it will be for a few weeks, but we won't be spending all our time under water. We're going to have some specialist training in one location, and then some serious rugby tuning up before the competition too. But I'll let you know all that in good time. Today is going to be a video day, so Kelly will talk you through the ins and outs of Sevens. Enjoy.'

CHAPTER 4

Kelly was everyone's favourite coach. She was serious and strict when she needed to be but was also up for a laugh and wanted the students to enjoy playing the sport. Kim also liked that she was very clear and direct in the way she handed out instructions.

'I'm going to presume that you all know what a game of rugby looks like? Fifteen against fifteen, egg-shaped ball, lots of pushing and shoving and grunting?'

The students nodded, although Kim noticed Ajit didn't do so very enthusiastically.

'Well what we're going to play is not very like that. The ball is still shaped like an egg, but Sevens is a much faster game with very little grunting.

'I'll go through the basics first,' she said, flicking to life a screen that displayed the positions in the smaller game.

'We only play for seven minutes each half, and only seven players are on the field at any one time. There are usually twelve or thirteen-player squads, but World Rugby have reduced the schools' competition to ten-a-side for this tournament.

'The scrums don't take very long as there's just three players, the prop, hooker, prop. In Fifteens Rugby the front row is usually packed with big, strong men or women, but in Sevens that's not nearly as important. Fast, mobile players are what's needed most, no matter what position they play.

'Then there's the scrum-half, who puts the ball in... then the out-half, centre and winger.'

'We play on the full rugby pitch, which means there's lots and lots of room, so the best sides are those who have developed the best skills and are the fittest.'

Kelly brought up a video file of a Sevens game played at a tournament in Hong Kong.

Kim had played and watched plenty of rugby but she had never seen Sevens before and was amazed at how fast the game was played, with the action switching from end to end.

'Look at this,' Kelly said, showing a loose pass which was intercepted and led to a try. 'There's almost no room for error like there might be in the Fifteens – there's not enough players to cover so if you give your opponent a free pass, and they're moving at speed, there's no time for the defence to stop them scoring.'

She hammered home a few points she wanted to make, such as 'Support your teammates at all times,' 'keep possession at all costs' and 'run fast.'

'It's a really simple game, and as soon as we get the full squad together we'll get deeper into tactics and plans.'

She let the video play out, pausing to explain some of the differences between Sevens and what Kim called 'real rugby,' such as drop kick conversions, and the side that has just scored getting to kick off from half way.

Jess was entranced by the fast pace of the game and how running seemed so important. She announced over lunch that she would be a winger, 'and probably a very good one too,' she added.

Kim noticed that Ajit was very quiet as they ate and asked him was he OK with everything.

Ajit shrugged. 'I don't think rugby is for me. I always thought it looked very violent and while this game looks less rough I'm not sure I'd be any good at it.'

Kim smiled. 'So many girls in my school had that attitude when we started playing. But the great thing about rugby is it has a place for all shapes and sizes, and being big and strong is even less important for Sevens.'

'You'd probably be a brilliant scrum-half,' said Joe. 'And Kelly seems to be a really good coach so you'll be taught exactly what to do.'

'OK,' Ajit said, making a great effort to smile. 'I'll give it a go, so.'

CHAPTER 5

Kim woke early next morning and dressed quickly. Out in the corridor, she grinned as she saw the door of the next dormitory open slowly.

'You just as interested in seeing our next destination?' she asked with a grin as Joe tiptoed out of the room.

Joe smiled back. 'Yeah, it's been really bugging me. I can't work out where we are from the map. There's literally nothing between Iceland, Scotland and Ireland.'

The two climbed the hundred steps up to the tallest part of their island-shaped submarine, a room built into the cliff face that formed one side of the craft. They peered through the portholes out into the gloom of the deep ocean, catching glimpses of strange, ugly fish as they flashed in and out of view.

As they watched, Joe noticed the numbers were getting smaller on the gauge showing the depth at which they were travelling. He pointed this out to Kim.

'400... 350... 300... 250...' she reeled off the numbers.

'We must be getting ready to surface.'

Sure enough, a voice came booming out of the loud-speakers in the corner of every room of the island.

'The craft will surface shortly. Please stow any opened liquids and make yourself seated until we announce it is safe to move around.'

Joe and Kim sat down on the bench and secured the seat belt straps across their hips.

'150... 125... 100... 75....'

The water outside grew lighter as the sun started to break through. Joe laughed as a particularly silly looking fish with huge eyes and enormous fangs bumped its nose off the glass window.

'I wouldn't be laughing if he turned up in our school's swimming pool,' said Kim.

As the island crashed through the waves to the surface a judder was felt right through it. Joe held tight to the side of his seat as the room was suddenly flooded with sunlight.

He unstrapped the seat belt and rushed to the window and was stunned to see that Atlantis had surfaced about a hundred metres away from an enormous rock that rose maybe twenty metres out of the sea.

'What on earth is that?' he asked.

Kim shrugged. 'It looks like a giant pimple on the ocean,' she suggested.

The loudspeaker crackled once again.

'Students please report to the classroom in ten minutes,' the voice said. 'And, by the way, welcome to Rockall.'

Kim and Joe described the island to their classmates while they waited for Luce to arrive.

'It's just a rock,' said Joe. 'It's not as tall as our island and it looks like there's a ledge on top where the seagulls can rest. But I can't imagine where this academy could be…'

'You'll find out soon enough,' said Luce, who had just arrived with an armful of bright orange life-jackets 'We're going on a little voyage.'

She led the five up the stairs and out into the cottage that was the only structure above the surface of Leap Island. Kalvin, the Atlantis handyman and goalkeeping coach, was waiting for them, carrying five large yellow raincoats.

'Hi, Kal,' said Jess. 'I hope you have my size – these look very big.'

They quickly dressed and, sure enough, Jess's raincoat was almost trailing the ground.

'You look like some sort of yellow monk,' chuckled Ajit.

Jess made a face and hitched up her coat before following Luce out the door.

The first thing they felt was the wind, which battered their faces and whipped seawater into their eyes.

The waters weren't too choppy, but Kim nervously eyed the distance between them and the mysterious rock. 'Are we sailing over there in those?' she asked, pointing at the three bright orange dinghies that Kalvin and the other crew members carried out behind them.

'We'll be fine,' said Luce. 'We have an experienced crew who safely handle the dinghies in far worse conditions than this. We'll be over there in less than a minute and you've all got safety equipment.'

Craig checked and tightened his lifejacket once more before he stepped into the craft alongside Kim and Kalvin switched the engine into life. Ajit, Joe and Jess hopped on board the second boat and followed close behind as the crewman steered towards the rock. Jess looked over her shoulder to see Luce piloting the third with a nervous expression on her face.

The two other dinghies reached the rock and paused to allow Luce to catch up. She steered her boat to within two metres of the sheer wall and waited.

Joe and Jess exchanged glances and shrugs. Joe pointed at the wall.

'There's a straight-line crack there, just above the water-line,' he showed Jess.

'It's widening,' she said, as the crack opened slowly. In less than a minute they could see the feet of people rushing around inside, and soon there was a two-metre square door-way in the rock.

Luce turned and shouted to the other dinghies. 'Be careful climbing ashore. Use the handrail.'

A light was switched on inside, showing the inside of a cave and a team of men dressed in green overalls. One stepped forward and beckoned Kalvin to bring his dinghy closer. Kim stood up and stepped across the narrow gap, grabbing hold of the handrail and using it to pull herself into the cave. Craig followed and Kalvin too, hauling the dinghy ashore behind him. They were joined by the occupants of the other boats.

'Ah Luce, my dear friend,' came a call from the back of the cave. A man stepped forward out of the gloom and embraced Luce.

'It is so good to see you again, and your students,' he smiled as he turned to face them. 'Let me introduce myself; I am the Warden, and you are all very welcome to the Advanced Marine Academy of the People's Republic of Rockall.'

CHAPTER 6

Kim blinked and looked around the cave. There was a stack of inflatable boats just inside the doorway; just in case of emergency she supposed. Otherwise the room was empty but stank of fish.

'What sort of school is this?' whispered Craig to Joe. 'And where are the kids?'

The Warden turned and walked towards the back of the cave.

'Let's get you out of those wet things,' he announced, leading them into a giant elevator. Kim noticed Jess was looking worried so she put her hand on her shoulder and smiled at her. 'We'll be fine,' she whispered as the cage descended slowly into the rock.

They all blinked again when the elevator reached the bottom and the bright lights hit their eyes. They were in a large chamber, the size of half a football field, filled with different types of boats and small craft. The Warden waved his arm with a flourish to show them the room.

'This is our humble college. We are a marine academy, so most of our work is in teaching our students about the ways of the sea and the various types of transport used on water. We have been here in Rockall for fifty years, training some of the greatest sea swimmers, rowers, sailors and yachtsmen and women the world has ever seen.'

Luce stepped forward. 'Thank you, Warden. Now let's get the students warmed up and we can talk a little more about the plan.'

One of the uniformed staff showed the students into a room where they could let their rain gear drip dry and they could warm themselves in front of a heater.

'This is a grim old place, isn't it,' said Jess when they were alone again.

'It's not very pretty,' agreed Ajit.

'Imagine being stuck here all the time under the sea with nowhere to go,' said Craig. 'At least we get to visit nice warm places when Atlantis surfaces.'

'I wonder what Luce's plan is?' asked Joe.

A knock came to the door and a tall youngster with blond hair stepped in.

'Hello,' he said. 'I'm Magnus Molloy. Are you the rugby

team?'

'Well… I suppose so,' replied Kim. 'Are you one of the students here?'

'Yes,' answered Magnus. 'I've been picked to join your school for this term. And I can't wait to get off this awful rock!'

'Why?' asked Joe.

'It's just so boring,' replied Magnus. 'We can't go for a walk anywhere, or even for some fresh air unless we're out on the boats. And then it can be pretty scary too outside – the waves are often huge.'

'Well I'm not sure it's a huge amount better on the submarine but we do have a cinema and at least we make our own fun going for walks in Beijing and London,' explained Kim.

Magnus looked puzzled, but they were interrupted by the door opening.

'Ah, Master Molloy, I see you have made the acquaintance of your new colleagues,' said the Warden with a thin smile. 'Let me explain a little to the Atlanteans…'

The Warden sat down, ran his fingers through his hair, and cleared his throat.

'Our school is home to twelve students who we train in the ways of the sea,' he began. 'We have forged links with other similar academies – such as yours – and have found interesting intersections in our work. We have been able to exchange ideas and technologies, and now we think it would be beneficial to have students travel between the schools.

'So, chatting to Luce recently, I heard about your problem with not having enough players to take up the invitation to the World Cup and suggested that we could team up to enter a combined team. We have identified five students with some interest or experience of rugby football, and they will be returning with you to Atlantis.'

The door opened again, and four students walked in, all wearing the deep blue uniform of their academy.

'Our students come from the maritime nations of the north Atlantic,' said the Warden, and we have one from each of the main ones here. There's Annie, from Scotland, Ferdia from Ireland, Sofie from Greenland and Rakel from the Faroe Islands. You've met Magnus, who is our Icelander. I think they'll bring something special to your school, and hopefully to your rugby football, too.'

When Luce had finished her words of welcome the

Warden snapped his fingers and two members of the staff came in carrying trays of hot drinks and some food. The students descended on them like jackals around an antelope.

'Great, sausage rolls,' said Craig, who bit into the pastry snack and instantly recoiled, his hand covering his mouth.

'That's not sausage,' explained Sofie, with a grin.

'Yes, everything we eat comes from the sea around us,' said Rakel. 'That's an eel roll. Very tasty.'

CHAPTER 7

Craig's face was still green when they skimmed across the water back to Atlantis with their new classmates. The Rockall students were amazed at the size of the island submarine – the flat area above the surface was big enough for a full-size football pitch and the rest of the island sloped upwards to the cliffs thirty metres above the sea.

It was still wild, wet and windy, so nobody stayed too long admiring the view, and Craig led the way straight for the white cottage that was the only sign of human settlement on the tiny isle.

As soon they were safely indoors, they shed their wet gear and after Kalvin had welcomed the newcomers, he led the way down into the living areas of Atlantis and straight to the dormitories.

'What's happened here?' asked Ajit as the boys went into their room. The Atlantis staff had been busy while they were away and the single beds that Craig and Ajit slept in had been converted to bunk beds.

'Hey that's not fair, how come Joe gets to keep his single bed?' asked Craig.

Kalvin frowned. 'I suppose because he's closest to the door. I don't think it's that big a deal anyway. You'll all have to muck in together for a few weeks and there's no sense arguing about this. Someone had to be the odd man out and it happened to be Joe. Nothing personal, Craig.'

Craig grumped anyway and lay down on his bed, making sure he put a claim on the bottom bunk.

'Do you mind if I sleep here?' asked Magnus, as he hauled his suitcase and kitbags onto the top bunk.

Ajit shrugged and pointed up top. 'Do you mind sleeping up there Ferdia? It's just I get a bit dizzy sometimes when I'm up high.'

Everyone laughed at the idea that Ajit would get dizzy less than two metres above the floor.

In the girls' bedroom next door, a similar conversation was being held. A new bunk bed had been shipped in, while Jess's bed had been adapted in the same way as Craig and Ajit's. Jess didn't seem to mind, though.

'Cool, does anyone mind if I take the top bunk?' she asked. Nobody objected, so Jess swung on the top bunk like a pommel horse and twisted her legs so they landed on the bed.

'I'd like the top deck too, if that's OK,' said Annie.

'We had a bunk bed at home when we were little,' said Jess. 'My big sister never let me sleep on top, so this is a brilliant adventure for me.'

'I suppose we're all happy now?' asked Kim. 'To be honest I'd hate to change, I really like this bed.'

She frowned for a moment. 'Do any of you snore?'

The three newcomers all shook their heads.

'That's OK,' said Kim, 'it's just that Jess makes enough noise to drown out the engines of the submarine.'

Jess threw her pillow down at Kim, who ducked and laughed as it hit the bathroom door.

'And that reminds me,' said Kim. 'We're always having arguments over who uses the loo every morning. We're going to have to be patient with each other and try to limit our time in there, especially if we're all rushing off to class or breakfast together. Maybe we could make a roster?'

Sofie looked at Rakel and grinned.

'A roster? Where we've come from you just join the queue – one shower between the twelve of us and two wash basins. I used to set the alarm for 6am to be sure the water would be hot. This is luxury for us!'

Annie climbed down from her bunk. 'She's right. Everything here is so new, and clean. And we won't need to wash as often if we don't smell of fish all the time!'

Rakel chipped in. 'It's lovely here, and more comfortable than Rockall. We won't be any trouble to you.'

'No, that's not what I meant, no one is any trouble to anyone else,' said Kim. 'You're all part of the team now so make yourselves at home and let's all try not to get in each other's way.'

'Rockall seems a bit grim?' said Jess.

'It's hard, true,' said Annie. 'But the sailing is fun when we get outside. We spend a lot of time in the gym.'

'Really?' asked Kim. 'They keep that to a minimum for us here, they say its not good for us at our age.'

'No, they have proper strength and conditioning coaches who record all we do,' said Rakel. 'I'm sure the Warden wouldn't allow us do anything dangerous.'

'Bing-bong,' went the loudspeakers, signalling a public

announcement.

'This is Luce,' she started, 'All students to the lecture hall in five minutes please.'

CHAPTER 8

Luce was waiting for them in the classroom. After a few standard words of welcome, she addressed the newcomers.

'I'm sure you are all enjoying your time on Rockall, and we hope you will have just as much fun here on Atlantis. We're a very different sort of Academy, and I'm afraid we have no boats for you to keep up your skills or even just to mess about in.

'As you know, you are here mainly to join our efforts for the Rugby World Cup, but while you are here you will have full access to all our facilities and training programs. We also spend three hours each day working on your usual school subjects, and we have organised for a YouTube channel for some of you to keep up with the subjects we do not teach here, such as Greenlandic and Faroese.

'We have some excellent rugby-specific coaches here, and also other coaches who will help you with aspects of your fitness and conditioning. But we also have a tradition in

Atlantis of looking outside the box, of trying to find new ways of approaching a sport. I'm sure if you ask him Joe will tell you all about the amazing techniques of Professor Kossuth and his theories about football.

'I've asked the Professor to study Sevens Rugby and he has come up with some interesting thoughts and worked out what exercises and sports would be useful to develop the skills you need. We'll be meeting him later in the voyage but the one thing he has decided you all should learn to become better rugby players is…'

Luce paused, and grinned widely.

'Speed skating.'

'Speed skating?' groaned Craig. 'I can't even roller skate.'

'How does that work?' asked Magnus.

Kelly, the rugby coach, stepped forward.

'I was just as sceptical as you are when I heard that first, but the Professor showed me how he thinks developing the skills of skating can help in rugby and I was soon quite convinced.

'You won't be competing at speed skating, so you won't need to learn the strategies, but it will help you in areas such as keeping your balance and control, learning how to get past opponents, as well as learning new ways to fall and how to accelerate quickly and stop safely.'

'How are we going to learn that here?' asked Kim. 'There's no ice rink on Atlantis.'

Luce smiled at her. 'The one thing you will all learn about this wonderful academy is that when we don't have something we find a way to make it happen. Our technicians have been hard at work to come up with a virtual Olympic-sized ice rink, just like those virtual golf courses you like going for your midnight walks on.'

Kim blushed.

'We will start here using roller skates – maybe Craig will finally master that skill – but we will be having a master class in speed skating by a former World Champion when we make our first stop in the next week or so.'

An excited buzz started among the children. Much as they enjoyed Atlantis, there was nothing like some fresh air and the chance to run around underneath a blue sky.

'Any questions?' asked Luce.

'Will it be warm where we are going?' asked Jess.

'No,' replied Kelly. 'And in fact, just to get you used to the weather where we are going, the temperature in the virtual rink will be set as low as it would be in the real world. So, wear your hats, gloves and warm clothing!'

CHAPTER 9

'I hope you don't mind me asking, but how come you have an Irish surname?' asked Joe as they walked back to their dorm.

Magnus grinned. 'At least there's people here who can pronounce it properly. Only Ferdia was able to on Rockall.

'My dad was a fisherman, from Donegal in Ireland, and during a storm his trawler was forced to take shelter in Høfn, on the east coast of Iceland. They were trapped there for weeks and he met some men who told him all the great stories about life fishing for cod inside the Arctic Circle. He was so excited by them that he quit the fishing boat and joined them.

'He met my mum too, on his first trip ashore and, well, you can fill in the rest yourself.'

'So how come you went to school on Rockall?' asked Ajit as he lay down on his bed.

'I've always been fascinated by the Icelandic sagas about men sailing or rowing tiny boats across the oceans to discover new lands,' said Magnus. 'Ocean rowing is a big thing where I live and I got pretty good at it, so the school suggested I take up a scholarship to Rockall,' he explained.

'Yeah, I was something similar,' said Ferdia. 'We live on an island off Galway and I got into currach racing when I was young – it's like a rowing boat but with a hull made of canvas and covered in tar. The races are good crack and St Brendan was supposed to have rowed a currach across the Atlantic to discover America. Can't see how he did that myself though.'

Ajit, Joe and Craig confessed to never having been on the sea in anything smaller than a car ferry until they first visited Atlantis, although Craig admitted to pedalling a giant swan around a lake when on holidays in France.

'And how come you played rugby in Iceland?' asked Joe.

'Well, I didn't really,' replied Magnus with a grin. 'My dad was mad about the sport and got a rugby ball shipped over for my birthday when I was about five. I loved that ball, and although at first it was only me and dad, after a while all the kids in school got into playing it in the yard. We used to gather in my house to watch the Six Nations and all these Icelandic kids cheered for Ireland.

'There's a bit of rugby in Reykjavik, but I never got in touch with them. It's funny, our language doesn't allow foreign words, so they had to make up a name for the sport – we call it *Ruoningur*. When the Warden told us your school was looking for kids into rugby I stuck my hand up.'

Ferdia looked at the floor as they Atlanteans turned to him. 'What about you Ferdia, at least you come from a country that's got a half-decent rugby team?' said Craig.

'Well…,' he replied. 'To be honest, I've never played it in my life. We play gaelic football where I'm from, and I never got a chance to give rugby a go. Even the nearest soccer club is miles from where I live. The Warden looked at me as the only Irish boy and presumed I knew what I was talking about. I threw in a few words I picked up watching Connacht on the telly and sure I got away with it, and I'm here!'

They four boys all stared at Ferdia, before Magnus slowly cracked a smile and they all burst out laughing.

'That's mad,' said Ajit. 'But I suppose you saw a chance of a nice holiday somewhere warm and went for it.'

'Somewhere warm? I wish!' replied Ferdia. 'From what Luce says it sounds like we're heading for the North Pole.'

CHAPTER 10

akel's head darted from side to side as they walked down the corridors towards the video room. Her eyes widened as she saw photos of the legendary sports stars that had preceded her and the rest of her new classmates. She marvelled at the pictures of them on Atlantis with backdrops in dozens of countries from South Africa to Hong Kong.

'I love the way your school travels around the world,' Rakel told Kim. 'I've only ever been to Iceland, which isn't exactly a sun holiday destination. The clue is in the name, Ice-land.'

'Is it colder in the Faroes?' Kim asked.

'Actually, it's a tiny bit warmer. Iceland is closer to the Arctic Circle.'

'At least you'll be used to the cold for this speed skating lark,' grumbled Kim.

They entered the video room, which to the newcomers was a great disappointment.

'It's just four brick walls and a wooden floor,' sighed Rakel.

'Just wait,' grinned Kim. 'There's more to this room than meets the eye.'

Luce arrived next, and called the group to order.

'First, I want you to try on these in-line roller skates, which come in all your sizes.'

She opened a box which contained bags labelled with each of the students' names and shoe sizes.

'How did she know what size we take?' asked Sofie.

'We have gathered a lot of information about you all which is important to how we go about our work. Having the right shoe sizes saves a lot of time and messing,' explained Luce.

The ten pupils tried on the boots and each marvelled at how perfectly they fitted.

'OK, settle down again please,' asked Luce. 'We are here in a full Olympic-sized speed skating rink, and as I warned you the temperature is about to drop below freezing, so zip up your fleeces and get on your bobble hats.'

Ferdia looked puzzled. 'What's she talking about?' he asked Craig. 'This is nowhere near the size of an Olympic rink.' Craig replied with a grin and pointed to the ceiling as the lights were dimmed.

With a flash, the room seemed to expand in size, as dozens of 3D video cameras trained on the room made it appear to be a vast aircraft-hangar-sized stadium with a shiny white floor.

Annie looked down, and the appearance of a skating rink seemed to fool her into thinking it would be slippery, so her feet went from under her and she landed on her bum.

'Ouch,' she called out, and was soon joined by Ajit, Ferdia and Jess.

'We've just sprayed a mist of coconut oil which helps replicate the slipperiness of the ice rink,' chuckled Luce. 'Be careful, and you'll be fine. It's all about learning how to balance on the skates and keep moving forward.'

The next ten minutes saw Craig fall to the floor at least ten times, but he kept trying and stayed upright for at least five minutes before his next fall.

'Nice one Craig,' said Luce as he gathered himself for another circuit. 'I've been watching and you seem to have got the hang of it. Keep practising and we'll have another session tomorrow.'

She turned to the group and signalled them to stop.

'Good work there, I see some accomplished skaters

among you, and the rest of you seem to have picked up the basics quickly, which is fantastic. You've earned a rest this evening, and you can all head back to your rooms now and get changed – we're going to the movies, and there may even be popcorn.'

CHAPTER 11

Kim munched on the salty snack as the superheroes saved the world on the big screen. She was a bit bored by the movie, and decided to catch up on her daydreaming, which she hadn't much time for lately.

From her seat in the back row her eyes wandered around the small cinema as the other nine students seemed transfixed by the screen showing grown men and women in shiny nylon costumes.

'They're a quiet bunch mostly, the Rockallers,' she thought. 'That place seemed so dull and strict, they're all afraid to say boo. I'd say they'll settle in and relax soon enough. Annie seems good crack, though. And Magnus.'

Just as Kim was thinking his name, Magnus turned his head around and grinned at her.

She turned bright red – 'Oh no, did I say that out loud,' she wondered – but her blushes were spared.

'Are you snoring?' asked Magnus.

'No,' replied Kim, 'I've just given up watching this rubbish!'

'Want to grab a cup of tea?' he whispered.

She grinned her reply and slipped out the side door of the cinema.

'That was complete tosh,' laughed Magnus. 'I hate the way they take characters from the old Norse and Icelandic myths like Thor and Loki, too.'

'I'd love to read a few of those stories,' said Kim.

'I have a collection of sagas in my room, I'll let you have it later,' Magnus replied.

The pair sat at a table in the canteen sipping tea.

'What do you think of Atlantis?' Kim asked.

'It's amazing,' he replied. 'It's not just the facilities and the amazing things like the cinema and the video room, but the whole atmosphere in the place. Rockall was very serious – there was no fun with the staff and everyone just told you to work harder at everything. It was really grim at times,' he said, with a frown.

'But this place seems to be the very opposite. Everyone seems so positive and helpful, and they really want you to be happy here.'

'Yeah, I know what you mean,' replied Kim. 'Luce can

have her moments but she's mostly very supportive. The canteen staff are lovely and Kalvin is just a giant softie. The teachers are great too, but some of them are a bit weird. It's a shame you couldn't stay here all the time.'

Magnus sighed. 'Yes, that has already crossed my mind,' he admitted.

'Well maybe if you become the star of our rugby team they might let you stay?,' wondered Kim.

'Ha, ha, it would take a lot more than that to impress the Warden,' replied Magnus.

'Why?' asked Kim.

'Well, he *never* praises anyone for anything they do, and only talks to the students when one of them wants to give up and go home.'

'Does that happen often?'

'All the time,' said Magnus. 'I've twice tried to get out but they've persuaded me I have to stay because they depend on the money they get from whoever pays for the scholarships. They tell you all the staff will lose their jobs and the kids will all have to go home and we'll never get let back into a normal school. It's heavy pressure.'

'And who pays the scholarships?' asked Kim.

'Nobody knows – or rather, nobody says,' he replied.

CHAPTER 12

The students spent the next three days learning more about rugby from Kelly and practising their speed-skating. The more Kim practised switching from foot to foot and swerving the more she started to understand how skating might help her at rugby.

As she zipped past Jess for the fifteenth time, Luce stepped into the video room and blew a whistle.

'Thanks all, that looks like a good session. I've been watching you on CCTV and talking to your new coach who's also been able to watch you on a link. He'll be joining us shortly, which is why I'm here to tell you that we'll be surfacing in about an hour, so I suggest you all clean up and meet me in the canteen for a quick bite and a chat about our next destination. And dress up *warm...*'

Back in the dorms, the students changed quickly out of their sweaty kit and into the fleece-lined tracksuits. Unlike Rockall, where they all wore the same colour, Atlantis students each had a different colour – so each of the newcomers had been given a set in the same five colours. As Kim slipped on her top, she noticed Rakel quickly taking something green out from under her pillow – a book, maybe? – and stuffing it down the back of her purple leggings.

Just then, a loudspeaker announcement encouraged the students to hurry down to the canteen, so Kim decided against asking Rakel about it.

In the canteen, Luce was already at the top of the table waiting for them, and each place was set with a steaming bowl of tomato soup and a sandwich filled with each student's favourite meat or cheese and some crispy lettuce and tomato.

'Yum,' gasped Jess, despite filling her mouth with an enormous bite of her sandwich.

'Yes, Jess, I'm sure it is delicious but maybe leave the comments until you're finished chewing?' suggested Luce.

The rest of the students chuckled, but Luce quickly called them to order.

'Thank you. In about twenty-five minutes we will be arriving on Spitzbergen, which is the largest island in the Svalbard archipelago.'

Magnus moved forward and sat on the edge of his seat.

'Does anyone know where that is?' asked Luce.

Magnus's hand shot up. 'Yes, miss, it is halfway between the north coast of Norway and the North Pole. The capital is the closest town in the world to the pole.'

'Yes, and that's where we are headed, Longyearbyen, which is about 78 degrees north of the equator. To compare, Dublin is 53 degrees and Reykjavik is 66 – and the pole itself is 90, so our next base will be as far north as humans have been able to live and work.

'Just outside the town we will meet Professor Odd Olsen, the world's leading speed skating coach, who has retired to Svalbard. We will be skating in the open air, on a track built on a glacier, so you must take care to be well suited up and never forget your gloves.

'There are several challenges about the place where we are going, so be prepared for a little hardship. The vegetarians among you will have to live on the stock of frozen goods and biscuits we have on board as nothing can be grown on Svalbard because the ground is always covered in heavy frost. You also aren't allowed die here – because they can't dig through the frozen soil to allow you to be buried here,' she grinned.

'Also, although it is evening time here, and you might expect the sun to start to set, that doesn't happen here. For the next while the sun will hardly set at all, maybe an hour or so, so get ready for permanent daylight. It's hard to get used to but you won't be here too long, maybe three days.'

Luce asked them had they any questions, and Craig was first with his hand up.

'I'm not a vegetarian, so what will I get to eat while we are here?' he asked.

'Well, we will return to Atlantis each evening so you will mostly eat in this canteen, and I'm sure Fleur and Maureen will organise some feasts with the local produce. As you might imagine, there's plenty of fish, but I'm told there are some local delicacies that you might enjoy.'

Magnus, Rakel and Sofie started to laugh.

'What's so funny?' demanded Craig.

'Nothing,' replied Sofie. 'It's just the food you're used to is hard to come by in these lands, so we eat what lives here, like you do in your land of cows and sheep.'

'So… what lives here?' asked Craig, 'not more of those eels?'

'Well, you can have eel,' said Rakel, 'but maybe you'd

prefer some seal burgers or some delicious reindeer stew?'

Craig's face turned green again, and he quickly left the room to the sound of laughter.

CHAPTER 13

After Luce had left to attend to Atlantis's imminent arrival in Longyearbyen, the students got chatting about their new home.

'You seem to know a bit about it,' Kim said to Magnus.

'Well, it's not that far from us, I suppose, just about 2,000 kilometres,' grinned the Icelandic student. 'My rowing club watched a video about a group of oarsmen who were the very first to row from Svalbard to Iceland. Our local hero, Fiann Paul, was the leader – he's a superstar back home.'

'What time are we getting into Long-barney-ear?' asked Jess just as the craft took a lurch and the loudspeaker crackled into life.

'Please take your seats and strap in, we are about to surface….' the voice called out.

Even the canteen seats had belts, so the kids just waited for the all-clear message and continued chatting.

'It's Longyearbyen, Jess,' chuckled Magnus. 'It's named after some American guy called Longyear, but everyone jokes that it also means 'the long year town.' Lucky for you it's only the long week town…'

The kids were quite relaxed, thought Kim as she looked around the room. Everyone seemed to be getting on quite well, and there were no problems so far. She wondered, too, whether that would last.

There was a lurch as Atlantis broke the surface, soon followed by the captain announcing that they had arrived in Isfjord, the inlet that led to Longyearbyen.

'We will be mooring a short distance off the town and will be bringing the students and staff across the water in a few minutes. Please bring your warmest clothing as the temperature is below zero, even though we are just coming into their summer. Take care and enjoy your stay here.'

The kids filed out of the canteen and up to the anteroom where Kalvin handed them their lifejackets. 'Wear your bobble hats too,' he called, 'and your sun goggles.'

When they had all done as they were instructed Kalvin tackled the locks and bolts that kept Atlantis safe from the outside world and swung upon the door. Even with the goggles they were dazzled at first by the blaze of white which clung to everything except the deep blue sea.

'Wow,' said Annie. 'We get snow in Scotland – but never like this.'

Kalvin stepped outside first and tested the temperature. He returned to collect their transport. 'All right now,' he said, as he hauled two dinghies down to the shoreline. 'Be extra careful getting in and out of the dinghy as you won't last long in the water in these temperatures. And no messing either as I won't be jumping in after you!'

After Kalvin's warning they crossed the short distance to the shore without any incident. Kim was in the second boat and stared at the snow-covered mountains that lined the fjord and the menacing icebergs that had drifted into the inlet.

'Do you have icebergs in Greenland?' she asked Sofie.

'We sure do,' she replied. 'Much, much bigger than these ones though. We sometimes go on a school trip to watch new ones breaking off the cliffs – calving they call it. It's beautiful but also scary because it shows that the ice is melting everywhere, which isn't good news for people who live near sea level because the water is getting a tiny bit higher every year.'

Kim stared down at the surface of the water, terrified that

the boat might overturn and pitch them into the icy depths. The journey was over before she could ponder that too much, and she was mightily relieved to plant her rubber boots on the hard, icy shore of Svalbard. They had landed about fifty metres from the edge of town and jogged on the spot until the last craft arrived.

'This is a lot different to our last training camp in the Caribbean,' she thought, sighing. 'Still, what an amazing opportunity to see the world.'

When all ten of the students were safely ashore, Luce stepped forward.

'All right everybody, we have a short stroll into town where we will introduce ourselves to the authorities and wait for Professor Olsen to arrive. You must all be careful in this new environment, which leads me to my final warning about Svalbard. This might sound weird, but it is actually against the law to travel outside the towns here *without* carrying a firearm…'

Kalvin opened his enormous furry coat and lifted out a rifle.

'But why?' asked Joe.

'Because,' answered Luce, 'on Svalbard humans share living space with… polar bears.'

CHAPTER 14

'**W**hy would they want to shoot polar bears?' asked Jess. 'That's barbaric. *And* they're so cute!'

'Well....' replied Sofie. 'They have been known to kill people. They have no fear of humans and they can run faster than us, so it's best not to get anywhere near one.'

'I have no intention of shooting a beautiful polar bear,' insisted Kalvin. 'But if one of them threatens a hair on any of your heads, you can be sure I'll be there to stop it.'

'But there's only about twenty-thousand of them left,' said Jess. 'I don't want Atlantis to be responsible for reducing that number.'

Craig and Ferdia had been trying to get a snowball fight started but talk of polar bears ensured the students were more interested in scanning the landscape to see if any dangerous creatures were camouflaged among the snowdrifts.

Luce's revelation also put a pep in their step and they travelled the short distance to the town hall in a very short time.

Longyearbyen was a strange little town, with lots of brightly coloured homes huddled close together as if to keep warm. The group were surprised at how few people were out on the streets in broad daylight, but Luce reminded them that it was the middle of the evening when everyone would be eating, drinking or watching television.

She led the way to the town hall and gave the main door a rap before pushing it open.

'Come back in the morning, we're closed,' roared a huge bearded man in a black t-shirt from behind the desk in the entrance hall, which was lit by a huge open fire.

'That's no way to welcome a cousin of Ragnar O'Reilly,' roared Kalvin in return.

The huge bearded man stopped, and peered at the Atlantean giant.

'Kalvin! Why didn't you say it was you,' said the Svalbardic sentry, who happily had lowered his volume. 'Come in, come in, and bring all your young friends with you.'

'You know this person?' Luce asked Kalvin.

'I do indeed,' he grinned. 'This is Stig Sorensen, one half of the greatest Norwegian Death Metal band I ever saw, Mammoth's Tusk. My cousin Ragnar was the other half.'

'So, my friend, what has you in Longyearbyen?' demanded Stig.

'These are the students of Atlantis Academy, where I work. They're here to learn about speed skating.'

'Ah from old Oddy Olsen no doubt?' replied Stig. 'Well he's the man for that line of thing, indeed. I still play a bit of music with him when the mood takes him.'

Kim was amused by this new character, who not only had the same build as Kalvin but had the same jovial character.

'So, you're all here for some skating?' asked Stig. 'Have you seen the rink Oddy built up in the hills?'

'No...,' replied Luce. 'Professor Olsen told me he had a rink here we could train on.'

'Well, he does, I suppose,' replied Stig with a broad grin. 'But I'll let him explain that to you himself. Now, please excuse my lack of hospitality, but if you would like some blubber soup I have a large pot on the boil.'

A few of the children said 'yes, please,' but Craig had learned his lesson and decided to investigate further.

'What's "blubber",' he asked.

'It's whale fat,' replied Stig. 'It's delicious, and has lots of good things in it like Vitamin D too. Do you want to try some?'

'Eh, no, I'll give it a miss,' said Craig.

'Seriously, it's a real delicacy back home in Greenland,' said Sofie.

'In the Faroes too,' said Rakel.

'Isn't whale fishing banned?' asked Jess. 'They're such beautiful creatures and lots of species are endangered.'

'In most countries, yes,' said Magnus. 'But in the countries of the Arctic Circle the whale can be an important source of food. They respect the species, though, and only catch one at a time and use every little scrap of it for food, heating oil, clothing and even carving its teeth.

'Very few plants can grow in some of the places we live and fishing can be hard too. I wouldn't eat it, but I can see why some people do.'

In the end, only Kalvin, Sofie and Rakel took up Stig on his offer – Rakel even asked for seconds, for later – and the rest helped themselves to the vending machine in the hall that sold sweets and snacks.

As they sat around chatting and munching, Kim wandered around the entrance hall looking at the photographs of the town's governors and scenes from its history. The town had grown up around a coal mining industry but now mostly made a living out of tourism and research. Anyone who chose to come here must be very hardy, she decided.

Her tour was interrupted by a loud banging at the door, which then swung open and a small, slight man stepped inside. From head to toe he was covered in snow, although you could still see his bright orange overalls.

'Ah, the rugby stars of the Atlantis Academy. Welcome to Svalbard. I'm Professor Olsen, but you can call me Odd.'

CHAPTER 15

'We couldn't call him anything else but Odd,' Joe whispered to Ajit. 'He's the strangest looking lad I've seen here – and I've only seen one other person, that giant hairy Viking.'

Ajit chuckled as the Professor shook the snow off his clothes.

'Bit of a blizzard kicking in tonight,' he told them. 'If it doesn't stop it might be best if you stayed here tonight.'

Luce frowned but Stig spoke up.

'Of course, you're more than welcome here. We have plenty of blankets and furs in our stores and I can keep the fire blazing all night,' the watchman added.

'Well, we'll see how we are in an hour I suppose,' said Luce. 'But I'm keen to get everyone back on Atlantis overnight.'

Professor Olsen slipped off his overalls to reveal a green velvet suit which stopped at the knee to reveal bright white high socks.

'He looks like a leprechaun,' whispered Jess to Ferdia.

The Professor climbed onto a bench and called the group around him.

'I'm delighted to see you all here, and I've been corresponding on the e-mail machine with your Professor Kossuth who has some interesting theories about how I can help you in your rugbying.'

Kim smiled and put up her hand to ask a question.

'Yes, young lady,' smiled Professor Olsen.

'Have you ever seen a game of rugby?' she asked.

'Not in the flesh,' he replied. 'But Professor Kossuth has directed me towards some videos on the U-Tubes so I have been studying it closely.

'From watching the Sevens style of rugbying I have learned that the better players are fast runners, but still rely on evasion more than speed to get past opponents. And in Sevens that almost always means a chance to score a trygoal.

'I understand now why my colleague has identified speed-skating as a useful weapon in the rugbyer's armoury and I will try to show you some of the skills you can bring onto the rugbying pitch.

'Tomorrow you will join me at my track, which is three

kilometres or so out of town. There we will have complete privacy and peace to conduct our sessions. I will leave now, but I will return here in the morning at eight o'clock to bring you to what the locals here call "Oddland",' he smiled.

And with that he was gone.

Kim and Luce peered out the door after him, but all they could see was his orange blur disappearing into the distance.

'The snowstorm is getting heavier,' frowned Luce. 'Even if it stops immediately it would be very difficult, maybe even dangerous, to get back to the dinghies and across the water to Atlantis.

'It might be better to stay the night in the Town Hall,' she sighed.

Kalvin had joined the watchman behind the counter where Stig shared stories of his life as a very loud rock star. Kim grinned as she watched Kalvin listening intently with his jaw hanging open. Her brother used to play that type of music when he was trying to annoy her so she knew how awful it was, but it still made her feel a little homesick.

'Time for bed, gang,' Luce announced at ten o'clock. 'Grab those blankets and furs and get as comfortable as you can. I'll be calling you at seven tomorrow so get some sleep.

If anyone wants to get up during the night call Kalvin or I.'

Kim collected a huge bearskin which she laid on the floor and wrapped around her. She was instantly as warm as toast, although a little guilty knowing it would be better if the fur was keeping its original owner warm rather than her.

Most of the students were still chatting away, excited by the novelty of a night away from their usual sleeping quarters. Ferdia and Craig were already asleep, while Ajit was snoring away in an armchair close to the fire. She spotted Rakel furthest away, with her back to the group, and noticed her shoulder seemed to be moving. She watched her for a few minutes and decided she must be writing or drawing.

'Can I wash my face before bed?' she asked Luce, who nodded and pointed at the door to the ladies' bathroom.

Kim stood and tiptoed her way through her sleeping companions, pausing as she reached Rakel. She peered over her classmate's shoulder and saw she was indeed scribbling away furiously. She looked like she was drawing a map. Kim coughed and said 'excuse me' as she passed by on her way to the washroom. On her return Rakel had put her notebook away, turned to face the other way and appeared to be asleep.

CHAPTER 16

Next morning, they were awoken by the sound of Luce banging her fist against a metal cabinet.

'Rise and shine,' she called out. 'This is your first day in the Arctic Circle and we have much work to do. I will call some taxis to bring us to Professor Odd's track, but first we have a special treat for you, thanks to Stig.'

'I have been up since five o'clock baking you some *kanelboller*,' the watchman announced. 'Now don't be frightened Craig, these don't contain any bits of animals or fish. They are our local speciality, buns with cinnamon and fruit.'

Craig was first to spring out of his makeshift bed, the hunger of a night without dinner propelling him to the front of the queue at Stig's desk.

'They're delicious,' he told his classmates after spluttering his way through a sweet roll in no more than ten seconds.

Stig had made fifty buns but the students polished them off just before the Professor poked his head around the door of the Town Hall.

'Good morning all, I hope you slept well? I was kept awake by a herd of reindeer braying all night so I'm sure you slept better than I did,' he told them.

After tidying away all the blankets, and thanking Stig for his hospitality, the Atlantis and Rockall students got dressed up for another day of action in low temperatures.

Outside they were surprised to see that the 'taxis' that Luce had called were in fact three snowmobiles.

'That's so cool,' said Joe. 'I've never even seen one of those things before.'

'Bags I don't have to share with Kalvin,' said Ajit.

'There are very few cars on Svalbard,' explained Luce. 'Everyone gets around on these snowmobiles, especially when they have to get out of town.'

The students piled into their transport before the drivers pulled away together and headed for the mountain that overlooked Longyearbyen.

Kim was just as excited as the rest of them as the snowmobiles scooted over the terrain and threw up flurries of snow as it went. As the journey got steeper she gripped the side of the vehicle and when they reached the top of the ridge she looked back over her shoulder at the brightly coloured buildings they had left behind.

'Wow, that's some view,' said Sofie, who was sharing the taxi with her. 'We have some brilliant snowscapes in Greenland but that's very special. I'm sorry they wouldn't let us bring our camera phones.'

Kim smiled, and nodded her agreement. Atlantis had taken their mobiles from them on their arrival at the island and never returned them. The school was very concerned about its secrets falling into the wrong hands and took enormous measures to protect them.

'That must be Oddland,' said Sofie, pointing down into the valley below which was empty except for a bright yellow barn and a huge patch of flat ground shaped like a running track, covered in ice.

'Oddland, yes,' grunted the taxi driver, who hadn't spoken a word on the journey up to then. 'Odd is *sprø*,' he chuckled.

The snowmobile stopped outside the yellow barn and waited for the others to arrive. Kim thanked the driver and ran over to Kalvin.

'What does *sprø* mean?' she asked him.

'Ah, you've picked some Norwegian, I hear,' he laughed. 'Well, it means crisps.'

Kim looked puzzled. 'The taxi man said Odd was crisps?' she wondered.

'No, no, no,' chuckled Kalvin. 'He may have said 'Odd is crisps' but that's a bit like you saying, 'Odd is nuts' – it means crazy in Norwegian.'

Kim smiled, and made sure her first word in the new language was filed away for future use.

When all the kids had arrived, Luce knocked at the door but there was no sign of the Professor. Kalvin went around the back but he was nowhere to be seen, but it was Ajit who first spotted something out of the ordinary.

'Look over there,' he said. 'There's something moving in the snow.'

Sure enough, something was throwing up flurries of snow a few metres from the back of the barn.

Luce warned the kids to stay back, and to be prepared to flee.

Kalvin approached carefully, getting ready to produce the rifle in case of wild animals, but he was relieved when the Professor's bald head popped up from out of the snowdrift.

'Ah, good morning my friends,' he announced. 'I was just having a quick snow bath after my sauna.' He moved to stand up but was interrupted by a shriek from Luce.

'Look away now, students,' she called. They all stared, allowing the Professor to dash back inside without anyone catching of glimpse of his far-too-wrinkly white skin.

'Sorry, Luce,' he called from inside. 'I don't usually get visitors so I forgot I was undressed. Give me a minute.'

The children checked out the skating rink while the Professor got dressed. It seemed huge, and they started to get nervous that this would be the first time they had used ice-skates instead of the indoor roller skates they had practised with on Atlantis.

Out stomped the Professor, again in his bright orange jump suit. He was wearing a pair of skates and jogged along on them through the snow until he reached the ice.

'So, here we are – this will long be remembered as the frozen field where Atlantis and Rockall learned how to win the Rugbyers World Cup.'

CHAPTER 17

Kalvin produced a box of ice skates that he had had made in each of their sizes. They hurried to put them on, not wanting to leave their toes exposed to the biting air for very long, even if they were well covered by warm fleece socks.

'Let's see what standard you all are first,' he suggested. 'I suspect some of you have plenty of experience on ice.'

True enough, Magnus, Sofie and Rakel zoomed around as if they were running in the school yard. The practice sessions on Atlantis had ensured that the rest were well past beginners' stage, and even Craig made a full circuit without falling, although he rarely got above walking pace.

'That's very encouraging,' said Professor Olsen. 'Now let's all try to go a bit quicker. Sofie, isn't it, would you mind leading them around at the pace you were doing earlier? Everyone else just try to keep up with Sofie. No racing now, I just want to see what speeds you're capable of.'

The Professor spent the morning helping to improve the basic techniques of the ten skaters, which by the time he had finished really impressed Luce.

'That's fantastic, Craig,' she said, after the Atlantean had zipped around for three laps without falling.

'Craig has done very well,' said Odd, 'he's shown the biggest improvement and we can now move to the next stage of our project. But first, lunch.'

He led the group into the barn, which was divided into areas for storing equipment and an area upstairs where the Professor lived. He brought them up the rickety staircase into a large room with a dining table covered with brown rolls, slices of pickled fish and salami, and more of those fruit buns that Stig had made them for breakfast.

'I also have a delicious pot of soup just ready for eating. It's full of the seafood we catch around Svalbard – mostly cod and salmon, so I'm sure you won't be too afraid of it,' he smiled.

The kids were starving after their morning exertions so they tucked into the feast. Even the picky eaters enjoyed everything, especially the tasty soup. While they ate, Kim wandered around the room looking at the photographs and framed items hanging on the walls.

'The Professor was a handsome chap when he was

younger,' said Luce, who was also interested in finding out more about the eccentric sports scientist. She pointed to a brown photo of a young Odd Olsen as he swished around the ice at some race or other.

'That looks like it might have been an Olympics or something,' she suggested. 'Those rings there look just like them.'

'Oh wow!' gasped Kim. 'It definitely is the Olympics – and look… next to it…'

There, in a tiny frame, was a small golden disc with the words 'Innsbruck 1976' engraved on it and the five linked rings that meant it was won at the Winter Olympics.

Professor Olsen noticed what they were looking at and walked over to them.

'Ah, you have seen my trophy of my finest hour as a sportsman. That was a glorious day, indeed,' he said with a smile.

'You won an Olympic gold medal?' gasped Kim.

'I did indeed, at speed-skating of course, for Norway.'

The Professor told them the story of his win, which saw him beat a Russian and a German into the minor medals, which made him a national hero.

'I kept skating for a while afterwards, but it wasn't the same with nothing higher to aim for. Some people aim for two, or three, or four Olympic golds, but I was content with being the best in my sport and decided to retire when I was twenty-three.'

'That was very young,' Luce replied.

'It was, but I had other worlds I wanted to conquer, such as finding out about the science of speed-skating and I knew if I could master that then I could find other young people who could take my research and turn it into gold. And I did. Almost all the skaters I've worked with since won Olympic medals,' he said, gesturing along a line of framed photos of athletes on podiums waving Norwegian flags. 'But then, well, the sport became *somewhat* uneven. Some countries will do anything to win and are happy to cheat. I became disillusioned with skating.'

'And what about other sports,' asked Kim.

'Well… I hadn't really thought about moving into other areas until Professor Kossuth wrote to me. So, in a few short months, I expect to have another photo up here, flying the flag of Atlantis and Rockall and waving the Rugbying World Cup.'

CHAPTER 18

Professor Olsen spent the afternoon showing the skaters how to improve their speed, and how to fall safely and stand up to resume skating.

'That was great work today,' he said as he signalled the session was at an end.

'Tomorrow we will put all this into practice for rugby, so bring your skating *and* your rugbying gear with you.

The students thanked their teacher and climbed aboard the snowmobiles for the thrilling downhill journey to the seashore. Kalvin retrieved the dinghies and they all made it back to Atlantis safely.

'That was a very exciting trip,' said Jess as the girls got back to their dormitory. 'But I'm seriously in need of a shower and a comfortable bed...' as she made a dash to be first to use the washroom.

'Me next,' said Annie, staking her claim.

'Fire away,' said Kim. 'I'm just going to lie down in my sweaty tracksuit that I haven't taken off in two days. If I don't wake up in half an hour please turn the water hose on me.'

She closed her eyes and images of their time in Long-yearbyen raced through her mind. She was still puzzled by something however, and slowly opened one eye to look around the dorm. Rakel was in the lower bunk of the bed nearest hers, and she was scribbling furiously. She looked up every few seconds to check no one was watching her, but seemed assured that they were all busy washing, dressing and dozing.

Kim kept her eyes closed as much as she could while still being able to see through the tiny slit. As soon as Jess came back into the room Rakel stuffed the notebook under her pillow.

Kim stretched and yawned and decided it was time to get up and get ready for dinner. She waited so she would be last in the queue for the bathroom but whatever chance she had of sneaking a look under Rakel's pillow was foiled by Annie and Jess insisting she watch them do a song and dance rou-tine they had been practising.

When they were all ready they left the dorm, but halfway along the corridor she pretended she had forgotten something so she could return there. She dashed inside and lifted the pillow on Rakel's bed – but there was nothing there.

'She must have moved it when I was in the shower. I wonder where she hides it?' she thought as she made her way to rejoin her friends in the canteen.

Between the fresh air, the non-stop activity, and the lack of food when they were on the mainland, the students were very, very hungry, and cranky with it. Craig and Ferdia jostled to be at the head of the queue.

'I'm not going to take it all,' snapped Craig. 'I'll leave plenty for you.'

Ferdia puffed out his chest and stood up to Craig.

'I was here first, it's a simple rule,' said the Rockall boy. 'Stop throwing your weight around to get your way.'

Craig went red and stormed off out of the room. His hunger got the better of him because he stormed back in thirty seconds later.

He was still waiting – at the back of the queue – when Ferdia walked up to him with two plates piled high with shepherd's pie and sweet potato wedges.

'I got yours for you when you got called outside,' he said, with a wink and a cheeky smile.

Craig stared at him, and at the plate of food, and grinned back.

'Thanks, mate,' he said. 'I'm sorry for the dramatics. I was just a bit "hangry".'

'Don't worry about it,' said Ferdia. 'It's been a long day. Now come here and tell me about this tennis lark. I've never had a chance to play it before.'

CHAPTER 19

The group arrived at Oddland a little late for the next day's skating class – 'Luce delayed us on purpose, she's terrified we'll see Oddy naked swimming in the snow again,' sniggered Jess.

Oddy was fully dressed and ready for action when they climbed out of the snowmobiles they had rented for the day.

'As you can see, I have brought the laptop out here so please be careful around it. Snow isn't good for its inner workings, I believe. I'll be showing you some moves on the U-Tubes that I want you to copy.

'Professor Kossuth and I have worked out what we call some *common goals* between speed skating and Sevens rug-bying. Endurance is important – in both sports you need to be able to move forward quickly for as long as possible, at times, so we will be making sure you get plenty of running done in the weeks ahead to build up good habits that your body can draw upon.

'The most obvious thing you notice about Sevens is that

hard, fast running. But lots of teams score tries by being clever when they have the ball and moving fast to switch it between players. I will show you my thoughts on how a player running at speed can evade a tackler running at them. Speed skating needs that type of ability to veer quickly one way or other, and we will learn the art of sidestepping and throwing a dummy pass.'

Kim, as the most experienced rugby player, was fascinated by what she was hearing, but some of the others were confused already.

'I'm sorry Oddy, but we aren't that up on rugby to know what a dummy pass is…' said Ajit.

'Oh dear,' said Odd. 'I'm not too hot on it myself, but I have made myself aware of the areas the Professor and I discussed.'

'Here, I'll show you,' said Kim, grabbing one of the rugby balls Kalvin had brought along for practise.

Kim showed how a player could shape to pass the ball one way, but not release it and go on running with it, or pass it another direction. Odd suggested that if a player looked one way and moved their hips to make it look as if they were going to pass, almost always the opponent would follow the pass. Oddy then showed the best way to twist your body to ensure you were able to spring away and find a gap and – hopefully – score.

'Here try it,' he suggested, lobbing the ball to Ajit and telling him to find a way past Joe. Now, because Joe was expecting the dummy, Ajit had to try to fool him by running past him first. On the fourth attempt he went to throw a pass, pivoted on his right foot and nipped around Joe's outstretched arms and raced off into the snow. 'Try for Ireland!' he shouted as he dived into a snowdrift with the ball in his hands stretched out in front of him.

Everyone laughed – even Joe – and Oddy asked him to show what he had done again in slow motion.

'No need for the dive this time though,' he smiled.

Ajit went through the move and just after he touched down he kicked the ball hard and high up the hill where it stuck in the snow at the top of the ridge.

'You make sure you run up and collect that when we're finished,' growled Kalvin.

The Professor asked everyone to try the move, and everyone found it came easy to them after a few practices.

'Now, it is important that you don't do this ALL the time

in a match. It works well because it fools your opponent that you're going to do something else. But if they think you're going to do it all the time then they'll adjust their approach and you're back to square one. Use it as just one weapon in your armoury, one you turn to now and again.'

The Professor next showed them how to approach a one-on-one situation, and the various ways you could twist your body to evade the tackler. He got them all to skate along the rink at him, looking for the best route around him. He showed them the types of swerves and sidesteps that would work and encouraged them to practise them while increasing their speed all the time.

Kim and Joe took a breather as the others tried the side-step drills.

'This is fantastic,' she said. 'I wasn't sure when Luce told us about this, but Professor Kossuth was dead right – this is so suited to some situations in rugby.'

'I know,' replied Joe. 'I can see how I could use it in football too. I can't wait to try it with a ball.'

Oddy's final exercise of the day was to show them the quickest way to fall and spring back up immediately. After trying it first on skates, the Professor asked them to change into their rugby boots to repeat the exercise.

While they were going through repetitions of running-falling-standing, Magnus took a breather to take a drink of water. As he swigged from the bottle he noticed something standing on the ridge above the racing track.

'*Sko, sko* ... I mean, look, look' he gasped before waving his arms to interrupt the Professor.

He pointed up the hill to where a large creature was looking down at them, and he called out as loud as he could.

'P-P-P-POLAR BEAR.'

CHAPTER 20

'There's another one,' said Ajit.

'And another!' screamed Jess as she rushed to stand behind Oddy.

Kalvin, who had been sitting on one of the professor's snowmobiles, strode out to the track and took charge.

'Right everyone, straight back to the barn, don't run and please don't scream or shout. With a bit of luck, they won't come near us but if they do then I'll be able to protect you with this,' he said, producing the rifle out from under his long coat.

'I have a rifle too, indoors,' said Professor Olsen. 'But we should be very reluctant to use them. They have no fear of humans so won't back off just because we use the guns. We will only use them in extreme danger.'

'There's loads of them,' said a terrified Annie, waving her arm towards the ridge where there now appeared to be at least ten bears of various shapes and sizes.

'They're probably just inquisitive about what we were

doing,' said Sofie, who had seen plenty of polar bears in her home on Greenland. 'They rarely attack unless they feel under threat.'

The group took refuge in the barn and gathered around the windows to watch the animals as they slowly made their way down the hill.

'We're trapped,' said Joe, checking how solid the walls were. 'I hope they don't decide to stay around all night.'

'Not another night away from my bed,' moaned Jess. 'And this place doesn't have a roaring open fire either.'

'I won't be sleeping a wink if those monsters are roaming around outside,' said Annie.

Kalvin and Odd were the last to come indoors, and the Professor looked quite concerned.

'I've never seen them behave like this before,' he told Luce. 'I just can't understand it.'

'Look,' said Ferdia. 'One of them is carrying something.'

Sure enough, something was locked in the powerful jaws of the largest of the bears.

'It's a rugby ball,' said Sofie. 'It must be the one you kicked up there, Aj,' she added.

'You must have woken them up,' said Jess.

'Ah, don't blame me,' said Ajit. 'Kicking a ball didn't make ten of those bears come down to see what we were doing.'

'Maybe they're hungry,' said Ferdia.

'Don't say that,' said Annie. 'Although there's not much meat on me so they might give me a miss,' she added, hopefully.

The Professor motioned to Kalvin and Luce, and the adults went into a smaller room at the back of the barn.

'What are they talking about?' wondered Rakel.

'I'd say they're working out which one of us they're going to throw out to the bears so the rest of us can make a break for it,' said Jess, with a frown.

'Really?' asked Ferdia.

'No!' said Joe. 'Jess is winding you up. I'm sure they're just trying to make a plan without people making stupid comments. This building looks strong and I don't think polar bears can use door handles. We should be OK until someone comes along.'

'Is there any of that lunch left?' asked Craig, 'I'm starving again.'

'There's plenty on the table over there,' replied Kim. 'He's just covered it up.'

'I need to wash my hands, they're stinking,' said Ajit. 'There was something sticky on that ball.'

'Really?' said the Professor, who had just returned from the meeting in the back room. 'Let me see.'

Ajit held out his arms, and the Professor sniffed at his hands.

'Seal blubber,' he announced. 'Very strange. That's the polar bears' favourite food. How on earth did that get onto the rugbying ball?'

Ajit shrugged his shoulders.

'It was one of the bag-full that Kalvin brought,' recalled Kim. 'I was using one too and it was a bit sticky at first before I wiped it in the snow.'

'I brought them from the submarine this morning,' said Kalvin. 'They were in the back of the snowmobile with Rakel and Annie.'

The two girls shrugged too.

'All very odd,' said Luce. 'Could someone have smeared the rugby balls with seal blubber as a way of attracting the bears?'

'Perhaps so,' said Odd. 'The polar bear has a very powerful sense of smell. It can scent its prey from over one kilometre away. And this stuff is very strong smelling so perhaps they came from even further.'

'But how are we going to get them away from here?' asked Sofie.

'I have a plan, but we must be patient,' replied Oddy.

CHAPTER 21

'The first thing you must know about polar bears is that although they look big and lumbering, you have absolutely no chance of out-running them. When they get up to speed they're much faster than even Usain Bolt,' said the Professor.

'They also have no fear of humans and have even been known to wander the streets of Longyearbyen.'

'So how are we going to escape?' asked Magnus.

The Professor looked at Kalvin, who looked at Luce.

'Well... we've been trying to contact the police down in the town but I haven't been able to get through,' she said, looking very worried. 'The Professor tells me that up here in the hills the communications are always breaking down. We will wait till morning and hope the bears will wander away.'

'And if they don't?' asked Kim.

'Well, we will wait as long as we can before we need to make a break for it. I have some ideas about trying to distract them.'

'Human sacrifice?' asked Jess.

'NO!' said Luce. 'Any that's not funny in this situation, Miss Jessica.'

Jess looked a bit embarrassed, but not at all sorry.

'OK, Luce. I just can't help trying to lighten the mood.'

'Well please don't until this is all over,' Luce said, sternly.

'I know it's only six o'clock and its bright outside, but we want you all to go to sleep shortly,' said the Professor. 'We'll keep trying to contact the police but if we can't then we will attempt to get you out of here during the night when the bears are resting.'

'But won't it be bright in the middle of the night too?' asked Sofie.

'Yes, you're right,' replied Luce. 'But the bears will be sleeping, we hope. It will also be better that we can see what we're doing and where we are going in the snowmobiles.'

The Oddland barn wasn't equipped for overnight guests, and there were no spare blankets or furs for the kids. Rakel, Sofie, Annie and Jess huddled together on the couch while Luce draped a couple of oilskin coats over them. Kim tucked herself into an armchair with an overcoat for warmth, but the boys had to sleep on the floor in front of the fire. The

Professor pulled shut the heavy blackout curtains which kept the daylight out. 'Leave your coats and boots on during the night, in case we have to make a quick getaway,' he warned them.

The adults stayed up for a while longer, going over the plan carefully and repeatedly. Kim found it hard to sleep and kept an eye open as their anxious voices discussed how to escape as safely as possible. Everyone else seemed to be asleep when the adults finally settled down and tried to get some rest, with Kalvin remaining on sentry duty to keep an eye on the polar bears.

Half an hour later Kim noticed stirring on the couch, and Rakel squirmed out from under the coats. She watched as she wandered down the back of the barn, and when Kalvin looked up she pointed to the bathroom. Kim decided she also needed a visit so she too headed for the smallest room.

The blackout curtains were very effective so the room was only lit by the log fire and the tiny corner of window through which Kalvin was peering. As Kim made her way to the back of the barn she noticed thin slivers of light coming between the cracks in the old wooden door.

When she reached the bathroom, she noticed that the

lightbulb was still switched to 'off,' confusing her as to what was causing the tiny beams of light. Did Rakel have a torch?

Kim sat on the chair next to the door and waited. The slivers of light continued to dance but now she could hear some gentle tapping and clicking. What was going on? Finally, she heard a tiny 'whoosh' noise that couldn't be anything but the sound of an email being sent.

The next noise came from the toilet flushing and Rakel opening the door.

'Oh, hi, Kim,' she said, flustered.

'Hi, Rakel, it's hard to sleep isn't it?' she replied.

'Yes, I really wish this was over,' she said, before returning to her couch.

Kim was back in her armchair a couple of minutes later and Rakel appeared to have gone back to sleep. With her mind racing, Kim stayed awake for another while, going over in her head what could have just happened. At the very least Rakel seemed to have broken the Atlantis rule about no mobile phones.

CHAPTER 22

Kim eventually dozed off and was having a nice dream about a warm, sunny afternoon at the beach when she was awoken by Luce shaking her by the shoulder.

'It's four o'clock, time to get up Kim, we're going to make a run for it,' she told her.

The rest of the students were stretching and yawning but as soon as they remembered what was ahead of them they silently prepared to depart. When Luce called them together there was little of the joking of the night before. They had all slept poorly, knowing the real nightmare wasn't in their heads, but just outside the door.

'Right now, we have no room for delaying or messing here,' she started. 'We need to get out of here quickly, into the snowmobiles, and as far away from here as possible.'

She explained the plan, and who would go in which snowmobile with which adult driver.

'But first, we must distract the bears. They haven't been sleeping much during the night, but four or five of them have just dozed off. We expect they'll wake up when we leave but we might be able to distract them and catch them off guard.'

'This is where you kids come in,' said Kalvin. 'We know the best way to distract the bears is with food, and the Professor has very kindly donated the contents of his freezer. We have some nice reindeer steaks and joints, and I wonder if any of you have done any discus or hammer throwing?'

Annie and Sofie put up their hands.

'I've thrown a few tennis racquets quite a distance,' said Craig. 'Would that do?'

Luce nodded. 'We also have the rest of the rugby balls, with their seal flavouring, so we'll need our best kickers for them. Kim, Joe… anyone else?'

Magnus and Ferdia put up their hands.

'Great, that should be enough, so,' she said. 'Each of you take a ball and kick it as far as possible over the track. Aim in different directions to split the pack up. The throwers will aim behind the barn, toward the mountains. Between them all that should tie them up until we get away.

'Everyone not kicking and throwing come with me and we'll take the snowmobile furthest away. The throwers will join the Professor in the next one, and the kickers should make their way as quickly as possible to the last snowmobile, which Kalvin will be driving.

'We will be making straight for the town hall as soon as we reach Longyearbyen. It's the only place that we can be certain is open all night – hopefully Stig won't have gone for a nap.'

Kalvin lifted his phone to show them. 'I have his number here so whoever comes with me can keep ringing until we get into range and he answers. Kim, can you look after that?'

Kim slipped the phone into her pocket and joined the kicking group at the front door where Luce was handing out the stinky rugby balls. The bears, most of whom were asleep, were gathered about fifty metres away at the side of the barn, so the Professor led Annie, Sofie and Craig around the back. He gripped a big leg of meat and motioned Craig to follow him. He swung it back around over his shoulder and spun around as fast he could, releasing the joint just as he came back to face the bears and launching it over their heads.

It landed with a thump in the snow. Two or three of the bears lifted their heads and trotted slowly back to where they had heard the meat land.

'Quickly now,' Oddy told the kids, and Craig hurled his joint twenty metres to the left of his effort. Annie and Sofie swung their steaks around like a frozen discus and they landed close to the remaining bears, while Oddy hurled a third joint in another direction.

'Go!' he told them, and they ran as fast as they could back inside and out the front door to the waiting snowmobile.

Meanwhile, Kalvin had been supervising the kickers, who punted the ball as far as they could – Ferdia kicked it furthest, muttering 'my old Gaelic coach would be delighted to see that,' as he leapt into the escape vehicle.

The bears were now all occupied with eating or chewing on the various treats that had been launched in their direction.

As Kalvin and the Professor secured the doors of the barn the rest of the kids scrambled into their seats. It was a tight fit, especially for the four wedged into Kalvin's vehicle.

'Hold on,' he called, as the last two snowmobiles pulled away. Kim felt her heart racing as she looked over her shoulder and was relieved to see that the bears were more interested in the actual meals in front of their noses than the potentially tastier ones that she and her classmates could have been for them.

CHAPTER 23

The journey down to Longyearbyen was uneventful. Kim was able to get through on the phone to Stig, who had the door unlocked and the fire roaring by the time they arrived.

'Thanks Kalvin, that was more comfortable than I was expecting,' said Joe as he climbed out and on to the pavement. 'That furry footrest was really warm, thanks.'

Kalvin looked puzzled as he chained up the snowmobile.

'Footrest? I didn't put anything in there.'

He peered over the top of the door to the back seats, and saw a furry white ball wedged under the front seat. He opened the door and lifted it out at arm's length, but got the shock of his life when a pair of eyes and a black nose uncurled from the furry ball, followed by a very sharp-looking set of teeth.

'It's a bear cub,' he screamed. 'How did he get here?'

'Ah, he's so cute,' said Jess. 'Can we keep him as a pet?'

'We most certainly will not,' said Luce. 'He's a wild

animal, and he will grow up to be a vicious predator. He's not going anywhere near Atlantis.'

'Can we call him Snowy?' asked Annie. 'He's adorable.'

The Professor stepped forward, with a very concerned look on his face.

'He must have climbed into the car during the night in search of warmth. But this is now very serious, a potentially dangerous situation,' he said. 'We did very well to escape the bears, but now the pack will come looking for their cub. And they will be able to track him right to this door.'

Luce looked terrified. 'What can we do?' she asked.

'The best solution is to bring him back up to Oddland, but that could be very dangerous too,' said the Professor. 'And we can't abandon him out in the wild or he could die.'

'Well look, you drive, I'll hold on to him in the back and we'll head back the way we came,' suggested Kalvin. 'As soon as we see the bears we'll let him out and scram as fast as we can.'

Professor Olsen nodded. 'That sounds like the best solution,' he sighed. 'We'll have to keep our eyes peeled so we see the bears at enough distance to turn the machine and get away.'

'I'll come too,' said Stig. 'I have good binoculars and can keep an eye out while you two are busy with driving and minding the bear.'

The students looked very concerned that Kalvin, Stig and Oddy were putting themselves back in danger.

'OK, but bring the rifle in case you are chased by the bears,' suggested Luce, and Kalvin patted the side of his jacket.

'I have it right here, but I'm more concerned this little lad will give me a nip on the way back.'

They climbed back into Oddy's snowmobile, which was the fastest of the three, and headed back up the mountain.

'We'd better go inside,' said Luce. 'If those bears come across country they might get here quicker than we did. They'll surely have noticed that Snowy has gone by now.'

Even though it was the middle of the night, Stig had been baking his delicious *kanelboller* and the students tucked in. No one was in the mood to go back to sleep, so they sat around chatting as Luce kept checking her watch.

After what seemed like two hours – but was probably just forty minutes – the door swung open and the three men stomped back in, bringing a blizzard in their wake.

Kalvin grinned broadly and gave them all the thumbs up signal.

'That was fun,' he roared.

The Professor took off his balaclava to reveal a face as white as the snow that was piled on his shoulders. Stig, too, looked a bit shaken by the experience.

'What happened?' asked Luce.

'Well, we met the bears just after we got over the top the ridge,' explained Kalvin. 'I dropped the little fellow into the snow, but as we were turning the snowmobile we got stuck in a drift.'

'Oh no!' said Sofie.

'Well, it was a bit hairy for a while, but the bears kept their distance. Little Snowy scarpered back to his Mammy and we stayed inside the car. They stared at us for a while, maybe a quarter of an hour, and then they just wandered off. I think they were full of reindeer steak so they didn't need to eat us.'

'And how did you get down here?'

'Well we eventually got it out of the snowdrift and got out of there as fast as we could. It started to snow on the way down – that look of terror on Stig and Oddy's faces is more to do with my driving than with any scary polar bears!'

CHAPTER 24

Luce announced that as Oddy had covered almost everything he had planned to, there was no point going back to Oddland. The Professor gave them a short talk on what they needed to work on, and promised to keep in touch over the internet.

'If you put some of these moves into action you will have every chance of beating your opponents in one-on-ones – and after that it's up to you whether you want to score tries or not. I look forward to watching you in the rugbying cup in Japan, although only over the live streaming,' the Professor added.

He decided he'd like to stay in town for a few days in case the bears were still hanging around up in Oddland, so Luce booked him into the best hotel with the grateful thanks of Atlantis Academy.

It was still only breakfast time, and Longyearbyen was just starting to come alive. Luce allowed the pupils out to do a little sight-seeing around the town and gave them each fifty kroner – about five euro – to buy postcards or sweets.

Joe, Kim and Sofie wandered down to the sea front and watched the trawlermen unloading their haul.

'That's the largest cod I've ever seen,' said Sofie to a grinning local fisherman.

'Baby *hai*,' he laughed back at her.

'What's that mean?' asked Joe.

'Baby *shark*,' smiled Sofie. 'I think he was joking.'

By ten o'clock the kids had all returned to the town hall and they bade fond goodbyes to Stig and Oddy. Kalvin gave them both enormous, bone-cracking hugs and was still wiping a tear from his eye as he led the students down towards where their dinghies were stored.

As they walked through the town, Kim remembered Rakel's visit to Oddy's bathroom, and decided she needed to investigate further.

'Are mobile phones banned on Rockall?' she asked Magnus, who was walking alongside with Luce. Rakel was just ahead of them in another group and Kim noticed her shoulders suddenly hunched and she half turned her head towards them.

'No,' Magnus replied. 'We are permitted to use them for

one hour every evening as we are so far from our families and friends it is good to keep in touch. But we were told that they are not allowed on Atlantis so we all left them behind on Rockall. We placed them in a special locker before we left.'

'Really?' said Kim. 'Everyone?'

Luce looked at her suspiciously, but said nothing.

Kim and Rakel both climbed into the dinghy that was piloted by Luce, and neither pupil said anything as they crossed Isfjord to Atlantis. Just before they reached the island, Kim noticed Rakel was fumbling in her pocket. She pretended to look away, but kept her eye on her fellow student. Rakel lifted her phone out of her pocket and with one swift movement dropped her hand over the side of the dinghy. Kim heard a tiny 'plop' and Rakel brought her hand back in.

Kim was stunned, but said nothing. She decided to see what else she could find out about Rakel before she brought it to the attention of the Atlantis authorities.

The kids were all tired and grumpy by the time they reached the academy, changed, had a proper meal, and returned to the classroom to listen to Luce.

'Right all,' she said, as they settled down. 'That was quite an unscripted stopover in Longyearbyen, and I apologise for the dramas that caused you to miss two nights in your own beds. However, I'm delighted you all got back safe and sound, and also Kalvin, to whom we owe a debt of thanks.

'My main concern is that the midnight sun and the early morning flight from Oddland has thrown your sleeping patterns totally out of kilter and we need to get you back in a proper routine as soon as possible. You may feel like going to bed now, but that would not be advisable. We want you to work through today – it will be a short day and we will have your meal early – and then go to bed no earlier than an hour before your usual bedtime.

'If you do that you should all sleep soundly and longer than usual, and then we will call you at the regular time in the morning. We will have a monitoring session tomorrow to check all is well and you are back in a normal sleep pattern.

'We will go over what we learned from Professor Olsen and go through his moves on roller skates and in rugby boots until they come as second nature to you.

'I'm afraid we will be remaining underwater for the next

few weeks – it's the Arctic Ocean after all – and Kelly will be putting you through your drills again. She's had a lovely few days holiday from you so I'm sure she's looking forward to working you hard,' she said, with a wicked smile.

'We have one more stop to make, to collect an extra member of the coaching staff, but otherwise we will be stuck indoors until just before we reach Japan. That will present its own difficulties, but please try to be patient and under-standing – it's the same for everyone so let's try and get on with each other.

'We are travelling off the north coast of Russia so we won't be able to surface for fresh air as it will be even colder and stormier than where we have just been. But you'll be glad to hear we have taken delivery of a large stock of provisions and essential supplies for the voyage, so there will be some fun items on the menu in the coming days,' Luce added.

'I hope you don't mean whale blubber and reindeer steaks,' said Jess. 'I've had more than enough of them to last me a long time.'

CHAPTER 25

Kelly had a huge grin on her face as she welcomed them back. Kim was delighted too – Kelly was her favourite coach, almost like a big sister.

'I hope you've all taken something from your time on Svalbard,' she started. 'I look forward to seeing you side-step and pirouette your way down the field when we get to Japan.'

The students laughed.

'I think we've a fair bit of catching up to do with some of you on fitness, so I'll get Chris and his team to come up with programmes for you all. We also have a lot to do with some of you on rugby. I'm going to spend the rest of the day going through the basics – we'll be watching a lot of video and I'll make sure you're all fully aware of the skills needed and the terminology we use before we take the next step. Now this might be a bit boring for a few of you – she looked at Kim – so if you want to find something more useful to do with your time you're more than welcome.'

Magnus put up his hand and explained how he had plenty of the basics from his time with Høfn RFC so he and Kim were both excused classes.

'What do you suggest we do?' he asked Kim after they had left the classroom.

'Let's head down to the video room and go for a run around Tokyo,' she suggested. 'It will get us in the mood for Japan.'

They had great fun for an hour, jogging around the city's streets and parks and trying to make sense of the jungle of advertising hoardings and neon signs that seemed to be attached to everything. They couldn't find a rugby stadium, so after an hour they switched off the machines and headed back to the canteen for a smoothie.

'It looks like an amazing city,' said Magnus. 'I've never seen buildings that tall before. I hope they don't have one of those earthquakes when we're there.'

Kim grinned. 'I think we've used up all our bad luck on that visit to Svalbard,' she chuckled.

Magnus sighed. 'Yes, that was a little scary at the end. I still don't know why the bears came looking for us.'

Kim frowned. 'What do you know about Rakel?' she asked.

Magnus stared at her. 'Wow, that's a bit of a jump isn't it?' he replied.

'Is it?' said Kim. 'She was in the snowmobile with the bag of rugby balls, wasn't she?'

'Yes, but so was Annie…'

Kim paused, unsure of how much she should share with Magnus. She decided to tell him everything.

After explaining about Rakel's secret scribbling, and the midnight email in Oddland, and the dumping of her phone, she asked Magnus what he thought now.

He stared into space for a few seconds and sighed.

'She's a strange girl,' he started. 'I tried to chat to her when we were on Rockall, but after six months I hardly know her. There's lots of links between Iceland and the Faroes and I know a couple of families that moved there but she wouldn't talk about the place.

'Then about a month before you arrived she went very quiet. No one could talk to her. Everyone was surprised that she was picked for this trip as she has shown no knowledge or interest in rugby.'

Kim frowned.

'I don't know what's going on, but I don't want to go to

Luce until I have more to go on,' she said. 'As it is it's just suspicious behaviour – especially dumping that phone.'

'Yes, and she's got rid of the evidence so it's just your word against hers,' replied Magnus.

'There's still that notebook, or whatever it is she's been scribbling in,' said Kim. 'I could try to sneak a look at it under her pillow.'

'But what if she catches you?' asked Magnus.

'Not if we go there now – she's still at class with Kelly till lunchtime.'

CHAPTER 26

Kim and Magnus walked along the corridor to the girls' dormitory. They didn't want to appear suspicious to anyone they met, and they were also aware there were CCTV cameras recording everything that went on in the submarine.

Kim slipped into the room while Magnus waited outside, ready with a story about waiting for his classmate to pick up something in case anyone came along.

She went straight to Rakel's bed and felt around under her pillow, but there was nothing there. She checked her bedside cabinet but that was locked. Finally, she lifted the mattress and found what she was looking for – a thin note-book with a black cover, with some strange symbols on it.

She riffled through the pages which were covered in a dense scrawl in a language she didn't understand. She picked out words she recognised such as 'Kelly,' 'Luce' and 'Atlantis' but was frustrated at not knowing how to read what she presumed was Faroese.

The one thing that she did understand however, was the drawing of the submarine, and the plans showing the inside of the Academy. All the rooms seemed to have been labelled and numbers showing the distance between each of them. She replaced the book under the mattress and left the room.

She signalled to Magnus to return to the canteen, and when they got there she recounted to him what she had seen. 'I need to get a look at that – Faroese and Icelandic are very similar, especially when they are written down.'

'Will we go back there now?' asked Kim.

'I suppose we…'

Magnus was interrupted by the noise of a siren coming over the loudspeaker.

'This is your captain speaking,' came a voice.

'The Atlantis needs to land to make some urgent repairs,' he said. 'We will be heading for a port called Belushya Guba, which is part of Russia, where we hope they have the parts we need. Please return to your rooms and don't walk around too much as we will have to increase our speed.'

Kim and Magnus both looked concerned and after returning their coffee mugs to the dishwasher, quickly made for their dormitories. By the time they got there Rakel and

Sofie were already sitting on their beds but Annie and Jess reckoned they preferred to be closer to the floor and were tightly clutching the sides of two armchairs. Kim went straight to her bed and tried not to look at Rakel, or her mattress.

'Anyone know anything about this Belarus Gubby place?,' asked Annie. Sofie and Kim shrugged, but Rakel had an answer.

'Belushya Guba is the capital of Novaya Zemlya, the long thin islands across the top of Russia. It's bigger than Ireland, but only a couple of thousand people live there, mostly soldiers and gas workers.'

'Full marks to Rakel,' laughed Jess. 'That's serious swot stuff.'

Rakel blushed. 'Ah, come on now, we do Arctic Geography in school so we studied it last term. It's basically the mountain range that divides Russia between Europe and Asia, extended out into the sea. I don't imagine there'll be much there that's any use to the captain, though.'

'He's in a hurry though,' said Sofie. 'I hope we're not in any danger.'

As if to answer her concerns, the dormitory door opened

and in walked Luce. Sofie repeated her question to her.

'That's fair of you to ask, as the captain did sound quite concerned, but he assures me there is no immediate danger to the craft or the people aboard. There is some issue with the ventilation that needs to be sorted out by surfacing and having a good clean. There are also some parts that seem to have malfunctioned that we will need to replace. Nothing to worry about…,' Luce added.

'I'm here to just reinforce the message that nobody should be wandering about outside their rooms and that you must stay here till we reach the port, probably around midday tomorrow. Dinner will be served here tonight, and we will be giving you some Academy work to do here in the morning.

'Is that OK? Any more questions?'

The five girls shook their heads and Luce turned to leave. Just as she was out the door she turned back and said, 'Kim, can I have a quick word? Outside here, please.'

Kim jumped off the bed and followed Luce into the corridor.

'What were you getting at with that question about mobile phones and Rockall yesterday?' she asked. 'It's been bugging me ever since. It seemed to come out of nowhere, which experience tells me means that it didn't. What's going on?'

Kim sighed. 'I don't know, honestly. I don't really want to say either as I could be being completely unfair.'

'Come on now, Kim,' said Luce, sternly. 'This is no time to be messing me about. Is there someone here with a phone that they shouldn't have?'

'Well no, not any more' said Kim. 'I did see someone with one but they threw it into the fjord.'

'Whaaaaat?' asked Luce, her eyes widening. 'That's very strange. OK, I won't press you on who it is right now but I will need to talk to you tomorrow. Now get back to your room and say nothing about this to anyone.'

CHAPTER 27

Kim lay back on her pillow and stared at the ceiling. She thought about the conversation and decided that she wouldn't obey Luce's order not to say anything – but the curfew meant she wouldn't be able to contact Magnus until the morning at the earliest.

She rolled over to put her back to the rest of the room and dozed off. During the night – her alarm clock said 4:43 – she woke up with a start. The engines were buzzing louder than she had ever heard them before and the room wasn't as dark as it usually was. She rolled over and saw a light glowed from under the duvet in the next bed – Rakel was reading, or writing, again.

'Is it a good book?' Kim hissed as she passed Rakel's bed on her way to the bathroom.

Rakel did not reply, but the light was turned out immediately. There were no signs of movement when Kim passed by again a few minutes later.

Next morning, as Atlantis continued its journey to the Russian islands, Kim and her friends worked in the dormitory with Kelly. The rugby coach showed them lots of videos of Rugby Sevens games, including all the best ones from the recent World Cups, for women and men.

'There's lots of moves that look like they've been worked out in advance,' said Annie. 'Will we be doing much of that?'

'We will indeed,' replied Kelly. 'Our schedule allows us about ten days in the region before we need to get to Japan, and that's when we will be doing all our full-pitch training and get to work out those sort of moves. We will be studying them here, and working on basic skills like passing and off-loading, but we won't be able to execute those big sweeping moves until we get onto a proper pitch.'

'Where are we going for that?' asked Rakel, a question that pricked up Kim's ears.

'Well… I can't tell you, or anyone, that just yet. We have a training camp being prepared but it's in quite an interesting place. Not that you'll have very much time for sight-seeing as I will be working you into the ground by then.

'Japan will be a bit of a culture shock for you guys, especially those that came from small towns or villages. It's so big, and fast…'

Kim interrupted to explain how she often took runs or walks around cities like Tokyo on the virtual-reality spinning machine.

'I've seen you do that – it's a really good idea,' said Kelly. 'I'll make sure we have Tokyo and Yokohama in the video system so you can take a look.'

'They're the two venue cities – they're only about 20 minutes apart but we'll be playing our pool games in Yokohama. If we get to the knockout stages we'll be moving into Tokyo. I'll show you the pools later in the week so we can start getting used to the shape of the tournament.'

Kelly looked at her watch and gently closed down the laptop.

'Right young ladies, we have to head to the canteen now where they'll give you a good meal. When we reach Novo…, eh, our destination, you're going to have to go ashore while the engineers have a look at whatever the problem is and get it sorted. So, again, get all your heavy coats, hats and gloves so we're ready to move when we drop anchor.'

The students gathered their gear and joined the boys in the canteen.

'That was pretty horrible being cooped up with that lot,' complained Ferdia. 'It was nearly twenty-four hours in there.'

'Oh, come on Ferd,' said Craig. 'You were as bad as the rest of us, and your feet are smellier too.'

'Do you lads ever use the shower?' asked Annie. 'It's the thing with a nozzle behind the glass door. You should try it sometime.'

The kids exchanged some light banter, but when Fleur and Maureen announced their all-you-can eat buffet was now open the talking stopped. Craig was first in the queue, piling his plate high with barbecued ribs.

'Leave some for the rest of us,' complained Ajit, but Fleur winked at him and showed him a second tray of steaming meat she had ready in case the first ran out.

The students devoured their meals, and sat back to relax afterwards, which was less enjoyable once Annie and Craig started a burping contest.

Kelly and Luce called by to tell them they were close to Novaya Zemlya and would be surfacing in the harbour.

'I'm afraid we may have to stay here for a night or two,' Luce announced. 'It depends on how the repair job goes.

We have you booked into a hotel, but there's one word of warning about this place, and it's a familiar one I'm afraid.'

'Not polar bears?' asked Annie, with a grin.

Luce frowned. 'Good guess Annie. You're actually right – there are lots of wild polar bears on this island and they have started to come into town to scavenge food. There will be no walking around town here, so we will have to travel everywhere in cars. You are going to be cooped up I'm afraid, but the hotel has a playing field attached so at least we can do some outdoor work.'

'What's this town like?' asked Sofie.

'You will see soon enough,' replied Luce, 'but don't expect it to be as much fun as Longyearbyen. Belushya Guba is a military town, so we have had to secure emergency permits for you all. We don't want you to go for walks outside the hotel and you must not misbehave in any way. I know that will be hard for some of you' – she smiled at Jess and Annie – 'but if you keep to the group we'll be in and out quickly.'

CHAPTER 28

Kim sat down beside Magnus and strapped herself in for surfacing.

'This place sounds a bit grim,' said Magnus. 'I hope they just allow us to stay in bed all day. I'm exhausted this last week.'

'No chance of that,' laughed Kim. 'Luce is a hard task-master. Oh, and by the way,' she said, lowering her voice, 'she tackled me about the mobile phone question I asked back on Svalbard. I told her how I saw it being dropped in the water but didn't mention Rakel's name. She's going to ask me again though. What should I do?'

Magnus chewed his lip. 'I think you have to tell her – and if she searches the room she'll find that notebook which could prove you're right.'

The captain interrupted again with a message that they were in the final stage before surfacing and expected to open the hatches in about ten minutes.

Kim lay back in the chair, closed her eyes and relaxed.

Living on a submarine was often a bit hard to understand but the act of surfacing and descending always brought it home to her. She could feel the craft rising in the water before there was a lurch as it broke through the surface and a wobble as it settled in the harbour.

Being inside the submarine for days on end made the stop offs very appealing, no matter how dull the destination promised to be. All the students jostled to be first in line out of the cottage into the fresh, bracing Arctic air. Kim stood behind Rakel who had her black notebook tucked into her overcoat pocket.

Craig, as usual, found himself at the top of the queue and barged his way out the door as Kalvin opened it. He stopped dead in his tracks.

'Wow, that's cold,' he shrieked. 'I could almost feel my saliva turn to ice!'

'Oh yes, I should have warned you,' said Kalvin. 'It's minus seven out there, so wrap up warm!'

Ice had already started to form on the surface of Atlantis, which was covered by a type of artificial grass. 'We'll turn on the undersoil heating so that doesn't get too dangerous,' he chuckled.

A small crowd of people, mostly soldiers, had gathered on the harbour wall to see the strange new arrival. They called out in a language Kim couldn't understand, and Magnus shrugged his shoulders when she asked him.

'I suppose it must be Russian, but I don't know that language at all,' he replied.

The students were quickly transported across to the quay by Kalvin, who didn't fancy being outdoors for long, and they were greeted by a bus driver who Luce had organised to ferry them to their hotel.

'*Privet*,' he said to them with a grin. 'Hal-lo.'

'*Privet*,' Kim said in return as she took her seat behind the driver.

The short drive through Belushya Guba let the kids know that Luce had been correct when she warned that fun would be a rare bird indeed in this town. All the buildings were dull – apartment blocks and office buildings and very few shops.

'I wish there were a few polar bears to be seen,' said Sofie. 'It might make the people look more excited at least.'

The hotel was just as anonymous looking, a low-rise block of grey cement with a sad looking neon sign over the doorway.

Kim stared at the lettering, which wasn't the same as she was used to reading and writing, but still looked familiar.

'What's that?' she asked Magnus, as they climbed down from the bus.

'Haven't a clue,' he said, 'but something in Russian, I guess.'

Kim frowned. She remembered where she had seen the letters before – but what was Rakel doing with a Russian notebook?

'Right students,' announced Luce. 'I'm afraid we have a little problem here. Because Novaya Zemlya is an island almost completely populated by military personnel, they're regarding our unplanned visit as some sort of invasion. They're being quite nice about it, but they're insisting that we stay within the confines of the hotel – which was our plan anyway – and that each of you undergoes an interview by the Russian secret service.

'We're not happy with this, and even unhappier that they won't allow an adult to accompany you for this interview. However, they have agreed that Kalvin and I can be stationed outside the room so if any of you feels uncomfortable just shout and we will come in.

'So, who wants to go first?' asked Luce.

Rakel put her hand up.

'I'll get it out of the way first, if you don't mind,' she replied, and made straight for the door of the interview room.

CHAPTER 29

Rakel spent about ten minutes in the room, and when she emerged Ajit went in next. The rest of the students gathered around to ask her what it had been like.

'It was simple enough,' she said. 'They just asked me my name, age, parents' jobs and, oh yes, what country I came from.'

'And that took ten minutes?' asked Magnus. 'Did you have to spell your parents' names out for him or what?'

Rakel blushed. 'They also wanted to know had I ever been to Russia before – which I hadn't. Anyway, he wasn't very chatty and took his time over every answer. Now, I want to go find my room, excuse me.'

As Rakel walked off, Kim noticed with dismay that the pocket in which she previously held her notebook was now empty.

She did see the book once more, sitting on the desk under the Russian policeman's left hand as he drummed his fingers on it during her own interview. Her spirits sank as she realised the last piece of evidence of whatever it was Rakel was up to was now gone. As soon as the policeman was finished with her she wandered off to find her room.

An hour later she was lying on her bed when there was a knock on her door.

'Hi, Kim,' said Luce. 'Can I come in?'

The Atlantis Academy manager sat down in an armchair beside the window.

'I'm sorry to disturb you, but I need to ask you again about the mobile phone and what exactly happened with it.'

Kim filled her in on how she had seen one of the students using the phone in Oddland, and later saw her drop it in Isfjord.

'And who was that student?' demanded Luce.

Kim paused. She had decided to tell the full truth, but still found it hard to point the finger at her fellow student.

'It was Rakel,' she answered.

Luce stared out the window, which had an impressive view of the town rubbish dump.

'Rakel. I'm not sure I would have guessed her,' she admitted.

'But, that's the thing,' said Kim. 'There's more to it than just the phone…'

She explained about the notebook and her midnight scribbles, and the maps, and the Russian lettering printed on the cover.

Luce's mouth opened like a goldfish as Kim explained where she had last seen it.

'On the secret policeman's desk?'

'Yes, which probably explains why she was so keen to go in first – and what took her so long in there.'

Luce nodded.

'I feel sick Luce,' said Kim. 'Sick that I was so close to hard evidence and let it go.'

'Don't beat yourself up,' said Luce. 'You couldn't have taken anything from her without getting into trouble.'

The manager stood and looked out the window again. She jumped backwards, startled, when she spotted a family of polar bears going through the rubbish in search of food. She turned back to Kim.

'I need you to promise that you won't tell anyone what I'm

going to say next,' she said, 'and that includes your friend Magnus.'

Kim blushed, and nodded.

'We are very concerned that Atlantis has been the victim of sabotage,' said Luce.

'Sabotage?' gasped Kim. 'But how… who…'

'That's what they're trying to find out now,' replied Luce. 'But there seems to be someone among us who has tried to – at least – slow our progress, and maybe even endanger everyone aboard Atlantis.'

'How…' asked Kim.

'As far as we can make out someone stuffed about ten toilet rolls into the ventilation shaft and set fire to them. It was during the night and it didn't affect the sleeping areas, but the crew on the bridge were choking on the smoke and got a terrible fright until they worked out what had happened. The fire also damaged the system and we need some parts to fix it.'

Kim was stunned. Could Rakel have done something like that?

'It now makes sense that she wanted us to come into port, so she could hand off her notebook to the first secret policemen she met,' Luce went on. She would have known the only place we could have landed was in Russia, too.'

'What are you going to do now?' asked Kim.

'Well, I'll have to have a chat with the captain and some other people to see what our options are,' Luce replied. We can't just throw her out here, and as you say, we don't really have any direct evidence that it was her. She kept away from all the CCTV cameras too, so I'm afraid we're going to have to keep her. But we'll need to keep a close eye on Rakel, which is where you come in, Kim.'

CHAPTER 30

After Luce left, Kim lay staring at the ceiling, going back in her mind over all the times she had seen Kim do something suspicious. She couldn't remember anything new, and nothing that she had observed of the young Faroese student in any way suggested that she might be capable of attempting to set fire to the submarine school.

She hopped up from the bed, and wandered downstairs to see if there was anyone about.

Joe was sitting in the lobby chatting to Ajit.

'I had a look at the field out the back. It's a soccer pitch, but it's very bumpy and worn,' Joe told her.

'Worse,' said Ajit. 'It's backing on to the rubbish dump which seems to be a feeding ground for polar bears. If we kick the ball over the fence I won't be going after it,' he laughed.

'You're not very brave – not like that Brazilian girl we played against in the Amazon,' replied Kim, reminding them of the time a lost football ended up being savaged in seconds by a shoal of piranha fish.

Ajit shrugged his shoulders. 'I'd prefer a nip from a half-inch fish than one from a half-tonne polar bear,' he answered, wisely.

They discussed how they might practise rugby on the pitch without cutting their knees on the hard, rutted ground, and hoped Kelly would come up with a solution.

'The goalkicker will have to kick towards the hotel, too,' said Kim. 'Which could mean a few broken windows. Who's going to have that job I wonder?'

'Jess got really good at kicking the football, remember,' said Joe. 'She was very accurate too.'

'You're right,' said Kim, 'but kicking conversions in Sevens is from a drop kick, which can be tricky to master. She'll need lots of practice.'

'She'll get all the practice she needs,' said Luce, who had just come back in through the front door. She sat down beside the kids.

'I've been talking to Professor Kossuth who has plenty of good ideas about rugby drop kicks. He's already identified Jess as the best potential kicker, and has worked out a programme for her to follow.'

The students all smiled, remembering the eccentric academic with his wacky theories about football that helped them to victory over a team of trainee professionals in the Brazil jungle.

'I'd love to see the Prof again, he was such fun,' said Kim.

'Well, your wish will be answered. He's going to fly in to join us before we leave this place.'

'When will that be Luce?' asked Joe.

'Longer than we'd hoped,' she replied, sighing. 'The parts we need are not here, so they're going to be flown over from Arkhangelsk in a couple of days – Professor Kossuth will be on the same flight, we hope.'

'So, we could be delayed even more?' asked Kim. 'We'll go bonkers in this place. Have you read the tour guides there,' she said, pointing at some sad looking leaflets on the counter at reception. 'There's one café, and it only opens for two hours a day.'

'Well you don't need to worry about cafés, now Kim,' Luce replied. 'This hotel is perfect for our needs, and we will be very well looked after. And remember what I said about wandering off – and if you need reminding just look over the fence at the polar bears.'

Kim smiled, thinly.

'Fair enough, but I need some exercise now. Anyone fancy a run? ... twenty times around the field – well, half of it, anyway.'

CHAPTER 31

Time dragged very slowly on Novaya Zemlya, although getting out onto the sports field next door was a useful break for the students of Atlantis. Because they had been cooped up for much of the previous few days, Kelly gave them plenty of physical work to do to get them moving.

Jess started practising drop kicks with Kim, who showed her how to drop the ball so that it would bounce just before her swinging boot connected with it. Her early attempts were comical, her kick first connecting before the ball hit the ground, then when it had already bounced and was wobbling away. But practice made almost perfect and within fifteen minutes she had mastered the basic kick.

'It's amazing how quickly you can good you get at something like this that you had never even tried before,' said Jess.

'I know what you mean,' said Kim. 'Like, gymnastics, and football, and skating. I'd never given any of them any thought really and now because of all the training and practice we're well capable of playing them in clubs. Being a full-time sports scholar is a great chance, isn't it.'

Kim smashed another drop kick over the bar from outside the twenty-two.

'Let's leave it there, girls,' Kelly interrupted at that point. 'Professor Kossuth will have ideas on what you should be doing next to improve your drop kicking. He should be here for tomorrow's session.'

Rakel was in a group working on passing with Deryck St Vincent, the tiny cricket coach from the Caribbean who seemed to be wearing five overcoats and two woolly hats. Kim sipped from a bottle of water and looked over at her, wondering who she really was and why she had done what she did. Twelve-year-old schoolgirls from the Faroe Islands weren't your typical spies and saboteurs.

Rakel looked across and realised Kim was looking at her. She stopped what she was doing and stared back. Their eyes locked for four or five seconds before Rakel turned her back and walked away.

Magnus tapped Kim on the shoulder.

'What's going on there?' he asked. 'Have you said anything to her?'

Kim sighed, and checked Luce wasn't about.

'I can't talk about it, Magnus, but I've spoken to Luce and told her what I saw. No one has said anything to Rakel but she definitely knows I'm on to her – that's why she ditched the phone and left the notebook with the cop.'

'Do you think you should ask her what she's up to?' he asked.

Kim shook her head. 'No, Luce has asked me to say nothing to anyone – even you. Actually, she mentioned you in particular, so she must have seen us searching in the room or heard us talking about it.'

'Us?' laughed Magnus. 'I didn't search anything. I was just your getaway driver!'

Even though the players were running around, the icy wind made it very uncomfortable and Kelly called the session to a halt early. She asked them to meet her in the hotel function room in fifteen minutes.

That gave them just enough time to take off their boots, get back to their rooms, change into a clean tracksuit and get back downstairs.

Kelly had a blackboard set up and was busy writing on it when they all made it to the room.

'This is the draw for the World Cup we will be competing in,' she said. 'And as you can see we're in a tough group.'

The rugby coach pointed to Pool B, where 'Atlantis-Rock-all' was lined up with 'France,' 'Australia' and 'Russia.'

'Hey, that's a bit unfair, isn't it?' said Ajit. 'They're, like, huge countries and we're just a rock and a submarine.'

Everyone laughed, but they also saw the truth in what Ajit said. The competition had all the usual suspects you see at big rugby events, but also tiny places few of the students had heard of, such as Tuvalu and Andorra.

'France and Australia will be hard,' said Ferdia, who had been reading lots of books about rugby in the Atlantis library. 'But we should be able to beat Russia.'

'I wouldn't be so sure,' said Kelly. 'The Russians have started to take rugby very seriously. Their team are actually all students at a full-time rugby academy they've set up in Moscow, and they've hired lots of Kiwi coaches. We need to treat them with respect.'

'But they're just going to be eleven- and twelve-year olds, like us, aren't they,' asked Jess.

'I suppose so,' smiled Kelly. 'It's all down to you kids, really. We'll set you up and give you all the best information and moves, but in the end there's just going to be seven players on the field at a time and whoever scores the most wins.'

Kim digested Kelly's words. Although few of the students had any experience of rugby, the coaches and staff seemed to believe strongly that they could mould them into a winning side. She still wondered quite how that was going to happen.

'When I was young I read the autobiography of a great American tennis player, and he wrote something that I always apply to my coaching. He said, 'Start where you are. Use what you have. Do what you can.'

'You ten kids have been thrown together. Only one of you was chosen because of how they played rugby,' she said, nodding at Kim. 'And she was picked because she really wasn't very good at it.

'But Kim showed an instinct, and a savage commitment to making herself better, that I knew I would be able to help. You have a long way to go still, but Kim will lead you brilliantly, and that's why Luce and I have decided she will be our captain in Japan.'

Kim was stunned, and went bright red, trying not to catch the eye of her teammates.

'Well done, Kim,' roared Magnus, slapping her on the back.

The rest of the students joined in with the congratulations, even Rakel, and Kim mumbled 'thanks.'

'OK now, settle down,' said Kelly. 'We've been able to get some video of the French and Australian teams in action in other competitions, so we'll study that and get you used to some of the things they'll try to do. I'm afraid we're very much in the dark as regards the Russians, but hopefully something will crop up before the tournament. Otherwise we'll just have to use what we have – and do what we can.'

CHAPTER 32

Next morning, Kim was up first for breakfast. It wasn't that she was in such a rush to devour the brown porridge called '*kasha*' that was served in big steaming bowls, more that she was fed up with the lumpy mattress and wanted to get out of bed before she developed bruises on her back.

She decided to give the *kasha* a miss and instead took a bowl of blueberries, a cheese sandwich and a glass of thin, watery orange-coloured juice that tasted nothing like the fruit.

She sat staring out the dining room window and thinking of the new responsibility that Kelly had landed on her. She was fine with it, really, and as she was the only one who had played proper rugby she reckoned she must have been the obvious choice. But she was worried that captaincy would affect her own game – now she had to worry that ten people were performing, not just herself.

She also realised that she had to solve her issues with Rakel – mainly because there was no way they could find an extra player at this stage. There were usually twelve in a Sevens squad, but that number had been reduced to ten for this competition. That alone would make it more demanding on the players as they would have less time to rest or take a break during games – and it would be almost impossible to field a squad with just nine players in the heat of Japan.

As she debated whether she would chance another glass of fake orange juice, she heard a commotion in the lobby, which was just beside the dining room. She heard doors bang and watched as the porter lugged two huge suitcases into the lift.

She heard a familiar voice say, 'Wait there, please,' prompting her to dash out to the lobby.

'Professor!' she called, before she stopped short.

Professor Kossuth was always an eccentric dresser, but this was his most amazing outfit yet. On his head was an enormous bearskin helmet, with huge furry flaps coming down to cover his ears and cheeks. His padded overcoat was equally out of proportion to his wiry body and made him look almost round. But the most extraordinary clothing was below the waist – the Professor wore his usual bright yellow shorts, finished off by woolly boots like a baby would wear, although they were much, much thicker.

'Shorts?' she gasped, unable to stop herself.

'Yes, yes of course,' he chortled. 'The knees are the gateway to the soul, or something like that. How are you – Kim, isn't it?'

Kim smiled at the favourite teacher she had ever had for any subject. Not only was he a wacky dresser, and a really sweet man, but he was also a genius who had turned the study of kicking into a science.

'Yes, Professor, and I'm sorry for saying hello to your shorts before I said hello to you.'

'That's quite all right, my dear,' he replied. 'I suppose my knobbly knees are quite a shock for anyone this time of the morning. You'll have to tell me all you have been up to since Brazil, but first let me get my room sorted – I'll join you for breakfast.'

And with that the Professor was off.

The rest of the students came down in dribs and drabs over the next twenty minutes, and all the Atlanteans were delighted to hear the Professor had arrived. Luce was doubly delighted.

'That means the spare parts are here too – I hope,' she said with a rare smile. 'I'll leave you here in the capable hands of Kelly and Professor Kossuth and get back to the Academy to see what's happening. With a bit of luck this will be our last breakfast here.'

CHAPTER 33

The Professor arrived down just as everyone was finishing their meal. He took a cheese sandwich from the buffet, removed the cheese and refilled it with porridge and blueberries, which he proceeded to munch as he wandered out to the playing fields.

'Goodness gracious, I don't like the look of the neighbours,' he joked, pointing at the polar bears who had come over to the fence to take a look at the hotel's newest, weirdest resident.

'It may be best if we play down this end this morning,' said Kelly, directing the players away from the creatures. 'The Professor will want to work with the kickers first so we'll keep our work simple and stay in this corner.'

Jess and Kim wandered over to the other corner of the field. Kelly had suggested to Kim that she also join in the masterclass as one never knew when the frontline kicker would be injured or unable to take a kick.

They looked over the fence at the bears picking through

the rubbish for food. Kim noticed that Jess's eyes were filling up with tears.

'It's so terrible about the polar bears isn't it,' she said. 'Global warming has so damaged their habitats that they have to scavenge for food here. I was watching a scientist on YouTube who said that within thirty years there will only be one-third of the number of polar bears there are now.'

Kim frowned. 'It's sad that we had to come here to bring that fact home to us. I'm really going to try to do something about it when I get home.'

'I know,' said Jess. 'All the food and packaging we waste is so damaging to our world, and its here that you see the creatures that are being hurt the most.'

Their kicking coach arrived to interrupt their chat. 'Let's see you have a go first, Jess,' suggested the Professor.

Now, although Jess had got the hang of drop kicking at the earlier sessions, she was a little nervous and fluffed her first attempt.

'Sorr-rry,' she winced before running to collect the ball.

'Don't worry about that, you'll take a few goes to settle in – which is why you always make sure to make plenty of attempts before every game starts, just to get in the groove.

Jess had another go and, reassured by the coach, she smashed it first time high over the crossbar of the football goal.

'Excellent,' said the coach, after she had repeated the success five times more. 'Now let's take a look at every aspect of your kicking and see all that you're doing wrong.'

Kim smiled to herself. Although Jess had made the conversions, the Professor would never be happy with just that. For him, a good kick was one where she had dropped the ball at the right angle, connected at the precise optimal spot on the ball, and kicked it with the right velocity. If all that was executed perfectly she would score 100 per cent of kicks, all precisely splitting the goalposts.

'The most important thing you must remember about Sevens is that you only have thirty seconds to complete your conversion after the try is scored. So there's none of this strolling back and having a drink of water and a chat for a minute or two – you must go straight to the ball and make your kick. Remember, you may have just run the full length of the field to score a try so your heart rate will be racing. You must try and slow it down and focus on the next job as quick as you can, without rushing it.

'Being able to cope with that sort of pressure is the difference between a good kicker and a great one,' the Professor told her.

'When we get back on to Atlantis I will make all sorts of suggestions for how you might position your body, or angle your foot. But really the key to a good drop kick is down to getting two things right.

'The first is the drop. A lot can go wrong with the timing of the drop, but if you can master it, a consistent drop will mean consistent striking of the ball.

'You must test out and practise on every new surface – they are all different and the ball's bounce will vary in very tiny amounts so get on to the pitch early and study how it bounces. See how hard and rough this pitch is, the ball bounces higher but is also likely to hit a rut and bounce off the opposite way to what you want.

'The next most important aspect is how you relax and balance your body, so you arrive at the perfect position to connect with the ball. Everything I've said this morning can be achieved by repetition, by hard work and by practice, practice, practice.'

Kim and Jess spent the next hour with the Professor,

working on dropping the ball so it bounced back exactly the way you want it. Kelly came over to see how they were getting on.

'I'm going to give them a break, Professor; do you want to come inside for a cup of coffee?'

Professor Kossuth nodded and so the adults wandered off, leaving the ten students to themselves.

'Who's your man?' asked Ferdia. 'He mustn't feel the cold if he wears shorts like that.'

'That's only one of the greatest football coaches in the world,' said Joe. 'He turned a ragbag five-a-side unit of beginners into a team that beat five trainee professionals from Brazil, who also had a crooked referee on their side. In my book that makes him a genius.'

CHAPTER 34

Training continued on into the afternoon, with all the players joining in as Kelly introduced them to some fast-paced tactical moves that might help them break down their opponents' defences.

'Your fitness levels have greatly improved after the last few weeks, but some of you are going to have to work on your stamina,' she said during a break for drinks. 'The games are only seven minutes each way but they're played at a much faster pace than 15-a-side and there's very little chance to get a breather. And on top of that, you'll probably be playing three games per day.

'So, it's going to important to get your diet right – we'll have a look at it when we get back to Atlantis as you've got into some bad habits here. Nothing major, but we need to get more nutrients into you. It's also important to keep drinking water and to get a full night's sleep.'

'It would help if we had our own beds to sleep in,' muttered Ajit.

'I heard that,' said Kelly, with a broad grin. 'And I'm glad to tell you that will be back in your own bunk beds in time for lights out tonight.'

That announcement got as big a cheer as if she had announced they were getting a day off classroom work.

'Luce has been in touch to say she will have a bus out the front of the hotel at six o'clock, so after this go and clean up and change and we'll all meet in the lobby.'

After a shower and quick change, it didn't take Kim more than thirty seconds to pack up everything in her room. She lugged her bag down to the lobby where she discovered she was first to arrive.

She was restless, however, and knew they would be confined to a cramped underwater home for the next week or two. She decided to explore the rest of the hotel's ground floor, starting with the long corridor that passed the function room. As she neared its end she heard someone sobbing, so she slowed down and carefully poked her head around the next corner.

There, in an area under the staircase, was an old-style

public telephone, but she was stunned to see that the person using the phone was her classmate, Rakel. She had her back to Kim, but she still thought it wise to hang back around the corner.

All Kim could hear was a mixture of crying and muttering in a language she couldn't understand. The one phrase Rakel kept repeating sounded like 'moe ear' but Kim hadn't a clue what was being said. After a minute or two she seemed to be winding up the call, and kept saying 'bye,' so Kim took the hint and quickly made her way back to the lobby.

Magnus and Ajit were already there, chatting about fishing, so Kim went to join Jess and Annie waiting just outside the doorway. They discussed how glad they were to be heading back to their own beds when a figure shot past them.

'Where's Rakel going in such a hurry,' asked Jess.

They watched as Rakel crossed the car park and ducked around the side of the building.

'Is she going to the sports field?' asked Annie.

'What could be down there?' wondered Jess.

Kim paused, and started off after Rakel.

'Tell Kelly where we've gone,' she cried, 'and quickly!' she added, as she disappeared from view.

As Kim rounded the corner she saw Rakel walking across the pitch towards the back fence.

'Rakel!' she shouted after her, making her classmate stop and turn around.

'Leave me alone,' she called back to her. 'You've caused enough trouble.'

'Wait! Wait!' said Kim, as she broke into a run.

She caught up with Rakel as she reached the back fence of the field, overlooking the town dump.

'What are you doing here?' asked Kim.

'I'm going to get bitten by a polar bear so I can go home,' she replied, tears flowing down her face.

'Why?'

'Because I don't want to be here anymore, I'm only here because they forced me to go.'

'Who? Who forced you?' asked Kim.

'The Russians!' replied Rakel.

CHAPTER 35

Kim put her arm around her team-mate's shoulder and started walking with her up the field towards the hotel. Rakel kept crying but hadn't said anything more by the time they were joined at the half-way line by Kelly and Magnus who had raced out of the building.

Kelly took Rakel by the arm and led her on to the coach which was parked outside the hotel. Luce, who had just arrived with Kalvin, joined her. Kalvin waited at the door of the bus and told the rest of the students to wait in the lobby until they were called.

The kids gathered around Kim and asked her what was happening, but she decided it was best not to say too much until she talked to Luce.

She went back inside to collect her kitbag, and Magnus followed.

'Was she really going to jump over the fence?' he asked.

'I don't think so,' she replied. 'But she might have been planning to stick her hand through it to get bitten. She really wants to get out of Atlantis.'

She explained about the phone call and what she had heard.

'Moe ear?' said Magnus. 'That sounds a bit like Icelandic. We say "*mooir*" – it means "mother".'

Although the kids were delighted to be getting out of Belushya Guba, the coach journey back to the harbour was subdued. Kelly and Luce sat up front, with the manager next to Rakel. As far as Kim could see they weren't talking, although Luce occasionally raised her hand to pat Rakel's shoulder.

Back on Atlantis they were quickly ushered into their dormitories and told to wait until the ship was clear of the harbour before they could come to the canteen. There were just four girls in their room however, and all they wanted to talk about was the mystery of Rakel's behaviour, and her absence.

'I wonder did she want to stay in that horrible town? She kept muttering about "the Russians",' suggested Annie.

'No way,' said Sofie. 'I think she was just fed up like we all were there. I can't imagine what I would have been like after another night in that hotel.'

Kim remained silent, her earlier mistrust of Rakel turning to concern for her welfare.

Later, in the canteen, it was the turn of the boys to speculate with even more off-beat suggestions.

'I wonder what the Russians want with her?' asked Craig. 'Do they want her to defect to play on their team?'

'Maybe they're starting a maritime academy and want her to reveal the secrets of Rockall?' suggested Ferdia.

'Or Atlantis?' chipped in Joe. 'There's a lot of very wealthy people in Russia these days. I've read how they've spent millions on big soccer clubs and are willing to do anything to be successful at sport.'

'But why would they threaten a young girl, if that's what they're doing?,' asked Ajit.

'I don't know,' said Joe, 'but when there's so much money going around there's always criminals looking to muscle in on the action. Sport is such a big business these days. Who knows how far they are willing to go.'

Magnus squirmed in his seat – knowing more than the others he was reluctant to join in the speculation.

The arrival of Luce helped them discard most of the theories, she didn't answer a lot of their questions.

'I'm here to tell you that Rakel hasn't been feeling well and I'm going to move her out of the dorm and into my own quarters until she's better. She'll start taking part in sports activities in a day or two, but until then she won't be taking meals in the canteen. When she eventually comes back I expect you all to be sensitive and not to mention what has happened in case it upsets her. Am I clear?'

The students nodded.

'Thank you. We have a movie lined up for you after dinner, so I hope you all get to relax and back in a better routine after the last few days. We're going to be aboard Atlantis for the next sixteen days and will have one more stop off before we reach Japan. I want you all to work hard and get yourselves into the place you will need to be for this tournament. Enjoy the movie and I'll see you in the morning for testing… Kim, can I have a word?'

CHAPTER 36

Kim was a bit taken aback – and could feel the other eight pairs of eyes burrowing into her back as she followed Luce out of the canteen. The manager led her into a small office and sat down behind the desk.

Kim sat in the seat opposite while Luce opened the folder she was carrying.

'All right, Kim, what I say to you between these walls must not be repeated to anyone. I think – I hope – I have got to the bottom of the problem of why Rakel has done what she did.'

'And what exactly has she done?' asked Kim.

'She has spied on us all – and for Russian criminals,' replied Luce.

'I'd sort of worked that out,' said Kim. 'But why?'

'Well, it was hard to get it out of her, not least because she is still terribly upset, but it seems her family has been threatened by Russian agents. They say they will hurt her mother if she doesn't do what they say.'

'Whaaaaat?' gasped Kim. 'Has she told the police?'

'No,' replied Luce, chewing her lip. 'They said if they told the police they would take other, more severe action. She's really terrified that they'll do something awful.'

Kim could feel her shoulders start to shake as she imagined the fear Rakel must be feeling.

'This seems to have all started a few weeks before we linked up with the Rockall students. Rakel's mother called her on Skype one night and told her that she had been visited by some agents from a foreign country, and she must listen very carefully. Her mother had a script in front of her which she read out, telling Rakel to volunteer for the rugby team, and that a parcel would be arriving with the next supply ship with a special notebook and a smartphone for her.

'The following week her mother came on looking more worried than before and read her out a list of things these agents wanted to know about Atlantis. She told her that she must use the notebook to write all these things in, and to draw maps of the layout of the submarine and provide as much detail as she could about what we get up to here.

'She was told to write it in Faroese so anyone who found

it couldn't read it and would think it was a normal sort of diary anyway.

'She was given the phone to make contact with them, and she had to email them photos of her notes and tell her how she was getting on. On Svalbard she realised you were on to her so they told her to dump the phone in the sea and to try to force the submarine to make land in one of the Russian ports, which were the only ones near where we were at that stage. So that's why she waited a couple of days before she set fire to that paper and stuffed it into one of the vents.

'But it was such a dangerous thing to do – it could have killed us all.

'That's also when they confirmed to her they were acting for the Russian team. They also knew that we would be interviewed by the secret police when we landed, so they told her to pass the notebook on to them with instructions where it was to be sent in Moscow.'

Kim's mind was reeling at the story that Luce was unfolding for her.

'The pressure was getting enormous on her, and she rang her father from the hotel tonight just before we left. He told her the Russian agents had called him and were very angry that she had been discovered. They told her father that she must resume spying and they would contact her when she got to Japan.'

'Poor Rakel, no wonder she was so upset,' said Kim.

'I know,' replied Luce. 'She's still very fragile and doesn't know what to do. We must look after her and reassure her that she's safe with us. Victor has people on the case who are trying to see who is behind it all.'

'Can I talk to Rakel?' asked Kim. 'I'd just like to tell her that I understand what it's all about and she would be very welcome back in the team. She was actually turning into a very decent winger and I'd love to have her in the team for Yokohama.'

Luce smiled. 'That's a great idea, it might help her. I'll set it up for tomorrow morning. Now, run along or you'll miss the start of the movie.'

CHAPTER 37

Kim and Rakel had a great chat. Rakel got very upset again, talking about her parents and how terrified she was for them, which only made Kim cry as she thought how easy it could have been for the Russian agents to have targeted her own mum and dad, or even her little brother. Rakel then tried to reassure Kim, which wasn't the idea of the chat at all.

The pair laughed, and hugged, and promised to keep talking to each other no matter what.

Over the next few days they became good pals, and the relief of sharing her burden with others showed in the improvement in Rakel's rugby. She was now a lethal finisher, and Kelly was very excited that she had nailed down such an important role.

'We have a very good side coming together,' she told Rakel after a training session one day. 'I'm itching to get them outdoors again, but we're still skirting the Arctic here so I won't be asking the captain to surface!'

Kim smiled. 'I agree, they are picking it up so quickly. But when are we going to be able to land? I really want a few lung-fulls of fresh air.'

Kelly checked her watch. 'Can you wait two more days? We have a landing coming up – weather permitting – in a rather interesting place.'

Kim was intrigued by Kelly's revelation, but decided not to share it with anyone until Luce announced it. The Rakel incident had made her a little wary of divulging secrets, although she completely trusted all her schoolmates.

She was enjoying her leadership role with the rugby team, and shared Kelly's confidence up to a point. Her main concern was that they had still not seen any action footage of their opponents, so didn't know what to expect when they got to Japan.

She decided to explore the Atlantis library, to see if there was any video of Sevens matches that might help them. Ferdia was already in there, buzzing his way through books on rugby and anything else he could get his hands on.

'I'd love to be on Atlantis all the time,' he sighed. 'The

library on Rockall consisted of two shelves, and most of them were just books of tides and sea charts. I love reading about sport, even games I don't know anything about.'

'I must confess I've hardly been in here,' said Kim. 'We got so much to read about sport for homework that I never read about it unless I have to. Is there much in the video section about the teams we're likely to come up against?'

'There were a few clips earlier, but I think Kelly checked them out for her research. But there's loads of stuff on other teams if you want to watch that?'

Kim spent some time watching the best players in the world in action, learning how they coped with the extra space and the challenges it brought. She was especially interested in the kicking techniques of the stars of the game and made a mental note to bring Jess in to watch how they did it.

'Is there an atlas here?' she asked Ferdia, who went over to a shelf and lifted a large book down for her.

'This is the best one they have,' he told her. 'It's very detailed – it even has my hometown in it!'

Kim opened the book and riffled through it until she found the pages that covered their current location, the north-east of Russia bordering on the Arctic Ocean.

'This must be the wildest, most remote part of the world,' she said. 'There are only a few towns and they look like they're very small.'

'I know,' replied Ferdia. 'That occurred to me when we were on the last two places we stopped. What on earth possessed people to come and live up here when there's loads of room further south where it's warmer.'

Kim smiled. 'Maybe they like fish?'

She traced her finger along the route she supposed the captain was following, past islands and towns with mostly unpronounceable names – she did get her tongue around 'Tiksi' and 'Pevek' – until she reached the narrow strait between Russia and the USA. Her finger went south then, all the way to the north of Japan.

'That's funny,' she frowned. 'If we're going to stop on the way to Japan there's actually nowhere we can, except Russia. Surely Luce won't want to do that after what happened with Rakel?'

Ferdia pulled the map closer, picking at what looked like breadcrumbs some previous reader had left behind.

'There's a couple of tiny dots in the ocean, but I presume

they're Russian too,' he said. 'It looks like we're going to be stuck inside this for a couple of weeks yet.'

CHAPTER 38

But Ferdia was wrong. As Kelly had told Kim, they had one more stop to make before they reached Yokohama, and it was in probably one of the strangest places on earth. Luce came to tell them in the canteen, the night before they arrived.

'Tomorrow morning we're going to be landing at the Diomede Islands, which are halfway between Russia and America in the Bering Strait. There are two islands, Big Diomede and Little Diomede, but no one lives on the big one, except Russian soldiers.

'America owns the other one, and about 150 people live there, making a living by fishing and carving walrus tusks into trinkets and jewellery.

'We're here because the man who owns most of the island is a great friend of Victor, the man who owns Atlantis. Victor's friend has great plans to develop Little Diomede as a place for tourists to visit.

'Now, you know the Atlantis has always been surrounded

in secrecy, and almost nobody knows about us and our programme. However, because we are taking part in the World Cup we will be getting more attention than before and Victor has decided to embrace it. He is concerned that the people who were trying to steal our secrets will try to do so again and so he wants Atlantis to be more open to the outside world and show we are a force for good. It will also help to stop the rumours that we are building some sporting super robots – yes, really, one newspaper wrote that last month.

'He has agreed that his friend can bring in a camera crew to film us practising for the World Cup and he expects it will get television coverage on every channel in the world.

'The island itself hasn't got enough flat ground for a pitch so we'll be doing all the rugby on Atlantis when we surface. The island is usually bound by thick ice but as summer is coming we have found a clear area just off the village so we will be able to come up there,' Luce explained.

'Will we be able to visit the island?' asked Ajit.

'I'm not sure,' replied Luce, 'it depends on the weather and what transport we can use to get over to it. We may be able to use their helicopter.'

'We won't be there very long – we are behind schedule because of the unexpected stopover so we will have to be in and out of Little Diomede in two or three hours. Wrap up warm, it will be very cold…'

'As usual,' muttered Ajit.

'Will there be a chance to do some skating on the ice?' asked Magnus. 'It would be good to get a last practice with the skates.'

'I'll see,' said Luce, 'I'm not sure how safe it would be. But it's a good idea.'

Next morning, the students got a rude awakening before their usual alarm call. The loudspeaker came crackling to life and the captain's voice came booming out.

'Good morning Atlanteans, and welcome to Little Diomede. We are currently just off the island and will be surfacing in a few minutes. So hold tight and enjoy your stay.'

The boys were slow getting out of bed and had to rush to get strapped in for surfacing.

'This better be over quick,' said Craig, 'I'm tired of these boring little islands.'

'Bring your ice skates,' suggested Magnus. 'Luce said we might be able to do a bit of skating. They won't need all of us for this film will they?'

The students devoured a quick breakfast before Luce came by to let them know what was happening. As she was finishing, she told them a little more about the islands.

'What I forgot to tell you last night was that the Russian island is only three kilometres away over the ice. The international date line runs between the two islands, which means its six o'clock *tomorrow* morning over there – we're almost a full day behind them!

'However, given our recent issues, I'm keen to keep away from the Russians, we won't be nipping over to see what the weather will be like tomorrow!'

Poor Craig was completely confused, and was even more baffled when they came up from the submarine and he could actually see the island where it was the next day.

The over-ground part of Atlantis was covered in a high-tech grass which dried instantly and had as true a surface as any of them had ever played upon.

Kalvin carried out his trusty remote control which he used to make a high netting fence spring up to surround the island, thus saving him from a dip in the freezing waters to collect stray balls. He pressed another button and two rugby posts sprang up from the turf, followed by a series of white lines appearing on the grass just where the perimeter lines, twenty-twos and half-way line should be.

'That's amazing,' said Ferdia, who hadn't seen the Atlantis pop-up pitch in operation before.

'I know,' replied Joe. 'He can bring up goalposts and nets with just one click, and he can turn the pitch markings to soccer too.'

'Stand back now,' warned Luce, as a helicopter zoomed into view and made straight for the middle of the pitch.

CHAPTER 39

A man with a microphone jumped out of the helicopter, followed by a woman with a camera over her shoulder. Luce walked out to greet them.

'And this has a submarine underneath? What an amazing set up you have here,' said the reporter.

Luce explained that she was going to get the students to run around and go through some rugby drills for the camera. She asked Kelly to run a proper session, reckoning that any sort of real practice outdoors was preferable to indoor training.

The players got a bit giddy, joking and messing as they threw the ball around and Jess practised her drop kicks.

Atlantis was moored close to shore, but the ice almost completely covered the channel and when Jess skewed one of her kicks high over the fence, she was able to step off Atlantis straight onto the ice and collect the ball.

The reporter interviewed Kim about what they did on Atlantis, and how they were preparing for the World Cup.

When he was finished he suggested they get some shots from above in the helicopter, and invited Kim and Luce along for the ride.

Kim had never been in a helicopter before, so it was an exhilarating experience as they swooped over the high cliffs of the island and back down to the town and the rest of the players going through their special moves on Atlantis, filming all the time.

While the helicopter was flying out over the ice, ready to make a turn back, Kim stared out the window at the vast expanse of frozen water across to the red buoy that marked half-way, and beyond that the Russian island.

'Look there's a polar bear,' she told Luce. 'It's lying down, I wonder is it sick?'

Luce stared down at the white furry creature below.

'I don't think that's a polar bear. Look, he's standing up now – and pointing something at Atlantis.'

Kim kept her eye on the furry beast. 'He's walking now, but that's not how a polar bear walks – it's definitely a human.'

The chopper landed safely, and Kim and Luce rushed out to tell Kalvin and the kids what they had seen.

'There's someone out there, and I think he's spying on us,' Kim told them.

Magnus and Craig had bunked off the last part of the training and were sitting putting on their skating boots in preparation for a quick spin around the ice.

Craig stared over at where Kim was pointing, and quickly opened the gate in Kalvin's fence. He set off on his skates towards where the spy was standing.

'Craig! Come back!' called Luce, but she couldn't be heard over the whirring of the helicopter's rotors.

The spy turned quickly and began to run back towards the red buoy. Magnus looked out as his friend was gaining on the unwanted observer in his white fur coat and helmet, and set off in pursuit. He was a lot faster on skates and soon caught Craig.

'This is crazy,' he told him. 'That's Russia over there. Once we're half-way across we're trespassing in Russian territory. There are only soldiers over there! They can shoot us!'

'He's only on foot,' gasped Craig, 'We can definitely catch him. You're faster, go ahead.'

Magnus shrugged his shoulders – Craig was right – so he stepped up the chase. He was very conscious that they were nearing the buoy on half-way but he decided to make one last sprint. He reached the spy thirty metres short of the red marker and decided the best way to stop him was to take him out with a rugby tackle. He skated right up behind him and took off, crashing into his back.

The Russian fell heavily into the ground and whatever he was carrying flew out of his hand and skidded off across the ice.

He roared something in Russian and struggled to stand up. Just at that moment Magnus remembered that the only people who lived on Big Diomede were military, and therefore this white furry spy could easily be armed. He turned and fled, zigzagging back across the ice in case the Russian decided to shoot at him.

As he neared Atlantis he heard the cheers of his teammates and waved back. The camera woman was busy filming him as he leaned back on the skates and shuddered to a halt, but she quickly turned away and began filming what was going on behind him.

Magnus turned to see Craig chasing him back to Atlantis, carrying something under his arm. An even bigger cheer rang out when everyone realised that Craig had snatched the Russian's camera off the ice before he could retrieve it.

The pair were submerged briefly in a mass of hugs from all their team-mates, but Luce quickly ushered them back onto the submarine. They bade brief farewells to the film crew, and the islanders that came out to watch and to present gifts of tiny walruses carved from the creature's tusks.

'Sorry about the rush,' she apologised. 'But in the circumstances I think it best if we make haste away from here. Thank you for your hospitality and I look forward to returning.'

As the students climbed down into the submarine, Craig stopped and put his finger up in the air. 'I get it now,' he laughed. 'I finally understood the whole international data line headache – I nearly skated into tomorrow, and almost didn't come back to yesterday,' he explained to Kim, suddenly looking very pleased with himself.

CHAPTER 40

B ack in Atlantis, time flew over the next week as the students practised hard for the tournament. Kelly went through the video of the French and Australian teams and suggested how they might counter their best moves. She also identified some weak links and came up with plans for how they might make that work to the advantage of Atlantis/Rockall.

'You keep calling us Atlantis/Rockall,' said Sofie during one classroom session. 'It's a bit of a mouthful isn't it?'

The class laughed, but Kelly nodded.

'You're right Sofie. I'm trying not to say just 'Atlantis' because this really is an equal combination of the two academies and I want to be fair to the Rockallers. If you can come up with a better name that would save time I'd be delighted.'

'How about Rockahantis?' giggled Jess.

'Sounds like a stupid princess,' grumbled Craig.

'Atl-all sounds like nothing, and it's hard to say,' said Ferdia.

'Atlarock?' suggested Joe.

'That's not bad, not bad at all,' said Kelly. 'I might use that. Now, back to work….'

Atlantis had their own scouts and coaches all over the world looking for video of the Russian team but try as they might they couldn't come up with any.

'I'm not too worried about that,' Kelly told them. 'You're all becoming very adept at the game and I'm sure you will be able to cope with everything they will throw at you. We will go through a variety of plans that can be used in every situation, but I'm sure you all have enough skill and are clever enough to work out what to do. We'll be with you all the way and you have a great team alongside you.'

After class broke up, Kelly asked Kim to stay behind for a short meeting.

'How are things *within* the group,' the coach asked.

'Eh, fine,' replied Kim, a little surprised by the question.

'Did Craig seem a little irritated by Jess?' she replied.

'Ah, we all get a bit irritated with Jess,' said Kim, with a smile. 'She always says silly things. But we all love her too. And Craig is always a bit grumpy. I think he gets homesick, although he denies it.'

'And Rakel?'

'Rakel's great,' replied Kim. 'She's really mixed well with the girls since the, you know, *incident*. I sometimes catch her looking sad, but she must be really worried about her mother and father. Has anything happened about that?'

Kelly shook her head. 'I'm afraid not. Luce is in touch with Victor's private detectives every day but they've very little to go on and they're trying to keep a low profile so the Russian agents aren't alerted to their presence. Hopefully the Russians will leave them alone now they know Rakel isn't spying for them anymore.'

Later that evening Luce came down to talk to the group in the canteen.

'This has been one of the most arduous campaigns ever undertaken by Atlantis Academy. The staff and crew have been brilliant in keeping us safe and keeping us moving, and with lots of hard work from your coaches and yourselves you have a great chance to do us proud in the Rugby World Cup.

'By doing us proud I don't mean we expect you to win

the trophy, but to play to the best of your ability and if that means winning, or losing, we will be very proud no matter what.

'Kelly has you in great shape, and the good news is that our long voyage is almost at an end, and when you next leave Atlantis you'll need sandals, not snow boots.'

Everyone cheered that bit of news.

Luce grinned down at them all. 'And better still, we expect to reach land sometime tomorrow. We will be sailing into Yokohama, and we will be staying there to prepare for and play in the first phase which starts in six days.

'So, make sure you get plenty of sleep and plenty of rest as I know Kelly has plans to make you work harder than ever before. And Professor Kossuth will be intensifying his work with the kickers – he has a new theory I believe, which as always with the Professor will be very interesting indeed…'

CHAPTER 41

There was a new air of excitement in the dorm that night, as everyone got ready for the next phase of their adventure. Sofie and Rakel were packing their bags already.

'I wonder will we be staying in a really nice hotel?' asked Annie.

'It couldn't be worse than the one on that Russian island,' said Jess.

'That wasn't too bad,' said Annie, 'It was more comfortable than Rockall anyway.'

'I wonder will there be a swimming pool,' said Kim.

'Or a sauna?' suggested Jess.

They all smiled and looked forward to settling into a more comfortable environment when they finally reached their tournament base in Japan.

The boys, too, were weary of living in the submarine, and they each found that sharing a living space with four others was less pleasant than sharing with two.

Ajit sat in an armchair in the canteen and closed his eyes. Kim sat down beside him and shook his knee.

'You OK, Aj?'

'Ah, I'm just tired of being cooped up in this sardine can,' he sighed.

'And…?' replied Kim, sensing there was more to it than that.

'Well, Craig for a start. He's really getting on my wick. He's always barging into the queue for the bathroom or breakfast. He knows he's a few centimetres taller than me and he loves letting me know it. And, to be honest, I'm not mad about rugby either. I do try hard, but I just don't enjoy it as much as you.'

'Why's that?' asked Kim.

'It's just not my game,' he explained to her. 'I grew up playing hurling and cricket, and a little bit of football, but rugby is very new to me and it's hard when you're a bit smaller than most of the guys.'

Kim was sympathetic, and she told him how she had struggled with the sport when she started playing. 'I was tiny, and I used to get pushed around by the bigger girls. But rugby is a game for all shapes and sizes, and you could be an excellent scrumhalf. You're fast on your feet, you've great hand-eye coordination, and you're very accurate every time I see you throwing any size or shaped ball. They're brilliant basic skills to start with.'

'Yeah, but Kelly has me out playing on the wing where there's not much to it except get the ball and run as fast as you can with it.'

Kim chuckled. 'That's a fair point,' she said, 'but there's an awful lot more to it than that. I'll have a chat with Kelly and see if she might use you in a different position.'

Atlantis made good progress during the night and it was just before lunchtime next day that the Captain came over the loudspeaker to announce they would shortly make land in Japan. The students changed into t-shirts and shorts and when the all-clear sounded they made their way up to the surface of their island.

The first thing that hit them was the blinding sunlight, then the wave of warmth that they hadn't experienced in many, many months.

'Hmmm, that feels good,' said Ajit.

'That's ridiculously hot,' said Sofie. 'It never gets this warm back home in Greenland.'

'There's also no polar bears,' said Jess, pausing, 'or are there?'

'No, there are definitely no polar bears,' said Joe.

'But they do have pandas, don't they?' said Annie.

'No, no pandas,' replied Kim. 'That's China, not Japan. My mum and dad are from China, although they never saw any pandas there either, they told me.'

'This is the most ridiculous conversation I've ever heard,' growled Craig.

'So says the man who thinks he went back in time just by skating past a red marker!' laughed Magnus.

CHAPTER 42

Atlantis finally came to rest off the coast of Yokohama on the north east of Japan's southern island, Honshu, and a small ferry came out to collect those staff and students who would be based on dry land.

There was an air of giddiness about, and even Craig was grinning widely as he looked at the high-rise modern city that would be their temporary home. The ferry sailed right up to and docked beside the hotel where they were booked to stay, and as a reward for a very smooth check-in, Luce told them they could wander the short distance up to the Landmark Tower which was one of Yokohama's tourist attractions.

'You must stay close to Kalvin, kids,' she insisted, however. 'Although Japanese people extend a warm welcome to tourists and crime rates are very low, there can be lots of dangers in a foreign city. I don't think any of you have ever visited a city this big – nearly four million people – and I'm afraid that although they all learn how to read and write

English in school, it is not a widely spoken language. Try to get used to the currency – it's about 125 yen to the euro – and be very careful crossing the traffic.

'Now, go out and enjoy yourselves for an hour, and keep an eye out for Kalvin. He'll be keeping a close eye on you!'

Kim took a card with the hotel's address with her, just in case. Joe, Ferdia and Craig just wanted to go to the pool and the rest of the bunch were still arguing about whether they wanted to go to the mall or not. Kim suggested to Magnus and Rakel that they just head towards the tower.

'It's impressive, but once you've seen one tower you've seen them all,' said Magnus.

Kim laughed, and walked on. She was just glad to be out of the submarine and having fun with the people she probably liked most of her team this year. It would be hard to say goodbye to them when the tournament was over.

'The shops are weird, aren't they,' said Rakel. 'They're a mixture of all those American brands, and then shop names that you can't read.'

'Well, I suppose that's the same when people go to your home country,' said Magnus. 'But now that you mention it, anyone fancy a burger?'

Kim winced. She did enjoy a tasty hamburger now and again, but the Atlantis nutritionist had recommended they eat certain foods – and avoid others – in the run up to the World Cup and she decided it would be best not to break her rules. 'No, I'm OK,' she said.

'You're just afraid that Luce will find out,' chuckled Magnus.

Kim made a face back at him.

'Yeah, you're right. But I also want to be able to run past those Australian lads next week. It's all right for you big lumbering forwards.'

The three wandered up to the tower and after checking out its impressive height, decided to visit the shopping mall at its foot. Magnus and Kim ducked into the first sports gear shop they found, an enormous supermarket-sized store with thousands of items of every item of clothing and kit for almost every sport you could name.

Rakel hung around the entrance for a couple of minutes but signalled to them that she was going to visit the bookshop across the hallway.

Kim found a pair of runners that she liked, and tried them on, before she remembered that Atlantis Academy provided them with all the kit they needed. She bought a Japanese baseball cap for her little brother and they left the store laughing.

Their laughter stopped as soon as they saw Rakel, however. Their friend was standing in the doorway of the bookshop staring at something in her hand. They rushed over to her, and saw it was a mobile phone.

'What's that?' asked Kim. 'Where did you get it?'

Rakel's lower lip quivered and she looked as if she was on the verge of tears.

'Look,' she said, thrusting the phone towards her friends.

There, on the screen, was a photograph of a woman crying, her mouth gagged and her arms tied to a chair.

'That's my mum,' said Rakel, tears streaming down her face.

CHAPTER 43

'Oh no, that's shocking,' said Kim, giving Rakel a hug. 'Your poor mum.'

'It looks like they're hurting her,' cried Rakel.

'They wouldn't want to hurt her, they've just tied her up to try to frighten you,' replied Kim.

'But where did you get the phone?' asked Magnus.

Rakel fought back the tears and pointed towards a bench that had just become vacant. They crossed the mall, dodging the local shoppers who were rushing past at great pace. They sat down and Kim put her arm across Rakel's shoulder.

'I was just browsing in the bookshop when this man put the phone on the shelf in front of me. I was a bit confused at that and looked at him, but he turned away quickly, saying, "Don't lose this one" in a deep, strange accent.

'He walked away then and I picked up the phone. The screen switched on when I clicked the button and this photo appeared. And that's when you came along.'

Magnus looked around but the mall was packed and the

man long gone.

'He must be one of those Russians,' she said. 'This means they must want me to start spying again.'

Kim nodded. 'You could be right, but let's talk to Luce about it. We could turn this to our advantage.'

Back at the hotel Luce was angry. She strode back and forth across the lobby, gathering her thoughts before she sat down in an armchair opposite the three students.

'You should never have split up, and Kim, you know especially that you shouldn't have left Rakel alone,' she said. 'They could have kidnapped her too, or worse.'

Kim looked down at the carpet. 'There was no way they would have done anything in a packed shop, Luce, and we were only a few metres away, anyway.'

Magnus also protested that they could never have expected the Russians to make a move against her in a neutral country, but Luce pointed out that was just what they had done to Rakel's mother.

Luce stood up and walked over to the window. She stared out at the busy harbour before turning back to the three students.

'I'd better get in touch with the Faroe Islands police,' she snapped. 'I'll get someone to go out and get Kalvin to bring the rest of them back. We need to lock you all down now, it's going to be high security from now until this tournament is over.'

Rakel ate dinner that night with Kalvin and Luce, who wanted to talk to her about what the Faroes police had said to her.

The rest of the students were very unhappy when they were told the new rules that Luce had handed down.

'But no one wants to kidnap us, surely?' said Craig, to no one in particular, as the rest of the students sat around a big round table to eat dinner.

'Well, I suppose what all this proves is that the Russians are taking this competition very seriously if they're trying to hijack our little team,' suggested Kim. 'We probably do need to be careful in case they decide to do something more direct against us.'

'But we're in a huge foreign city, we can't just stay in bed all day?' said Joe. 'We'll have to go out for training for starters, and then there's the matches next week.'

'Yeah, and there seems to be a lot of fuss about the competition too,' said Jess. 'Did anyone see the big banners in the shopping centre? It looks mad to see 'Atlantis/Rockall' up there beside 'England' and 'New Zealand,' doesn't it?'

'I suppose so,' said Kim, 'but they all have the same number of players and they're all the same age as us too. We've nothing to be afraid of.'

'Except armed Russian spies who might sneak up on us in bookshops, I suppose,' sighed Annie.

CHAPTER 44

The training sessions were amazing but would have done nothing for Luce's concern about the safety and security of her students, thought Kim. They were held in a local school, and hundreds of the pupils turned out to watch them, and it became quite hard to concentrate when every time you did something like a long pass, or an accurate kick, the crowd would burst into applause.

Kelly took charge of the sessions but also roped in Professor Kossuth to continue to work with the kickers, and also Deryck St Vincent.

'I want to work with you on your footwork now,' the tiny West Indian told them after a break. 'I know you've been working hard on turning those speed skating tricks into useful skills on the rugby pitch, but I want to work on what you do when you're in a tight corner, and how speedy footwork can get you out of awkward situations.'

The coach got four players to surround him, at a distance of two metres, but with a blindingly fast shimmy of his hips and a tricky looking dance move with his feet, he was outside the circle in half a second without any of them laying a hand on him.

'How did you do that?' asked Ferdia.

'Practice,' chuckled St Vincent. 'But it's not hard to train your mind and feet to work in that way. Does anyone here know how to skip?'

Craig, Ferdia and Sofie put up their hands.

'Good, well that's a start. Skipping can be tricky to master at first but I expect you will pick it up very quickly. It's great for your footwork, and your balance, which is why boxers use it so much. It's very good for general fitness too, and you can do it in your own bedroom.'

He handed Craig, Ferdia and Sofie a skipping rope each and invited them to show him their skill. He was impressed and sent them over to Professor Kossuth while he taught the rest of the kids how to skip.

The Professor smiled at the three, who smiled back as he had removed his yellow tracksuit to reveal he was now wearing a striped woolly jumper and lime green shorts, topped off with a bright orange baseball cap.

'You've all climbed ladders, I presume?' he said.

'Only up the top bunk in the dorm,' Ferdia replied.

'Well that's fine,' answered the Professor. 'The ladders we are using are horizontal ones,' as he rolled out some white plastic in the shape of a ladder. 'I've one for everyone here, but I'll first show you what I'd like you to do.'

The coach took one step back and then raced along the length of the ladder, taking care to step only on the grass between the rungs. 'This will help you measure your paces and help you improve your agility. We'll do it with one foot, then two feet, then sideways. You'll pick it up quickly and you should then realise how useful it can be.'

He set the kids loose on the ladders and they raced through the drills, getting better every time. After ten runs they had mastered the footwork, and the coach told them to sit down and rest before doing another set.

'Just like the skipping, this will help you out of tight corners, which often arise in rugby.'

The training session got harder as the day went on, but Kelly kept driving them. 'I know you're all fading, but remember we are going to be playing three matches a day. You will need to have the stamina needed to be at your very best for the last of those matches. One of them, of course, could even be the World Cup final.'

The kids smiled, and nodded, before throwing themselves back into the punishing exercises.

As training ended, there was another surprise for them, and almost as exhausting. The school's head asked could her pupils meet the Atlantis/Rockall players and they were soon swamped by the excited kids.

'Signing autographs is a real pain in the arm,' said Ajit.

'Yeah, it's like doing a hundred lines in school,' Ferdia added, wincing.

CHAPTER 45

Newspaper photographers arrived the next day, and more students, and even more came to watch the day after that. By the end of the week there were over a thousand spectators at the sessions and Luce had to announce that the players wouldn't be able to sign any more autographs because their hands were sore.

'That's a rare complaint,' joked Magnus as they rode back to the hotel in the bus. 'I'd never signed a single autograph in my life before this week.'

'I always thought it would be cool to be famous and have people ask you for your signature,' said Sofie. 'But now I'm not so sure.'

'OH MY GOD!' called out Jess, and everyone turned to see what had alarmed her.

'LOOK!' she said, pointing out the windscreen of the bus. 'IT'S KIM!'

And sure enough, there was Kim, or rather KIM!

The face of the Sevens captain was printed on a giant

banner which was hanging down the full length of a ten-storey building, emblazoned with the words 'KIM, Captain, Atlantis Rockall' and 'RUGBY KIDS WORLD CUP.'

Kim went bright red and buried her face in her hands. 'That's so embarrassing,' she muttered.

The rest of the kids were delighted though. 'That's really cool,' said Magnus, 'you're a total celebrity now in Japan. You might even get on TV.'

Luce laughed too. 'I think you could be right Magnus, in fact there's a TV crew back in the hotel waiting for us…'

Luce wasn't joking, but she was wrong when she said there was '*a*' crew. There were no fewer than four television cameras outside their hotel, and even more reporters all waiting to talk to Kim and her team-mates – in Japanese. They got some help from an interpreter, but the captain was still exhausted at the end of the interviews. She went straight to her room, which she was sharing with Rakel.

'That was horrible,' said Kim, as she plonked herself down on her bed.

'I know,' said Rakel, with a sad expression on her face. 'I

just hope I don't have to go on TV if anything happens to my *mooir*, sorry, my mum.'

Kim jumped up and hugged her friend, telling her not to worry.

'I know, I know,' replied Rakel. 'But the police back home don't seem to be able to find her. It's not as if the Faroes is such a big place.'

'They're working on tracing who took the photo they sent you on that phone, so maybe they can find out something from that?' suggested Kim.

'I hope so, but we haven't heard any more from the police or the Russians,' she replied, waving the phone that she now carried everywhere with her, even at training.

There was no contact by the evening before the tournament kicked off, and Rakel had decided to concentrate on the Sevens and put everything else out of her mind. She didn't want to let her team-mates down, especially as Kim and Kelly had shown such faith in her, even changing her plans to ask her to share the scrum-half duties with Jess.

Luce had organised a function room in the hotel which

they called the 'team room,' where they could hang out in the evenings and play video games or just chat. Kim tried to be there as much as she could, so she could talk to all her team-mates and make sure they were OK.

On that last night Luce and Kelly called a meeting for all the squad and coaches in the team room. Kelly went through the tournament schedule, which told them where they would be for every minute of the next two days. They would be kicking off against France at 10.07am next morning, with the game against Australia at 1.42pm, and the last pool game, against Russia, at 5.02pm.

'The top two in each pool qualifies for the quarter-finals, which will be held the day after tomorrow,' explained Kelly. 'The teams finishing third and fourth play in a plate competition so there will be plenty of games for all teams.'

'It's very strung out, isn't it?' said Joe.

'Well yes,' answered Kelly, 'but I think you'll be glad of the rest between games as it will be very hot in the stadium.'

'What's with the funny times?' asked Sofie. 'Nobody ever said, 'I'll see you at seven minutes past ten."

Everyone laughed, but Kelly pointed out that with so many teams and players – and a television audience all over the world – it made a lot of sense that everyone knew their timetable so the day was divided up in little twenty-two minute chunks to allow for a short warm-up, two seven-minute halves, a half-time changeover, and a quick handshake with the opposition when it was all over.

'So, don't dilly dally after it's all over or you could find yourself playing for Wales against Fiji!' joked Kelly.

CHAPTER 46

Kim and Rakel both found it hard to get to sleep that night.

'I'm always nervous before exams, or a big match,' Kim explained.

'I usually have no problem,' said Rakel, 'but I'm terrified that the Russians will do something tomorrow before the match.'

'I suppose so,' said Kim, 'but try and put that game out of your mind. Focus on what Kelly told us about France and Australia and that will distract you. I know that doesn't help you get your mum back, but it will at least help you to get to sleep.'

Rakel smiled thinly. 'Thanks Kim, you've been really great about all this. I hope I can repay your confidence in me tomorrow – and the next day.'

The girls eventually fell asleep and were only awoken next morning by the 7am alarm call that Luce had organised for every member of the squad.

'Why couldn't she have made it a 7.07am alarm?' asked Rakel. 'We could have had a tiny lie-on and we'd be up exactly three hours before the first game.'

Kim laughed and hopped out of bed. She had her game-day bag packed from the night before, so she just put on the green and blue tracksuit that they had been given to wear for the opening ceremony.

Downstairs at breakfast the mood among the players was excellent. They loved their new tracksuits and the amalgamated crest of Atlantis's classical columns over the isolated rock of Rockall was a big hit. Half of them had even been out for jog around the hotel grounds, less to warm up their muscles than to show off their new kit.

But by the time they were on the bus to the ground the atmosphere was more subdued. There were huge crowds packing the streets leading to the stadium and according to the bus driver the attendance would be more than half of the 72,000 capacity. None of the Atlantis or Rockall students had expected the tournament to be anywhere as big as it now appeared and several of them seemed struck silent by pre-match nerves.

Luce stood up at the front of the centre aisle and smiled

down at them all.

'This is what sport at the top levels is all about. It's about remembering and executing all the skills you learned back on those tiny, empty fields with just you, your coach and a dozen of your pals. Or in a cold sports hall in the middle of November when you're trying not to trip over the skipping rope.

'You bring all those things you learned, and you practised, and you take them out, outside here in front of a big crowd and big opponents. And everything you've learned is like an extra weapon, so don't be afraid to use some of those tricks Oddy taught you back in Svalbard, or Kelly showed you and made sure you practised fifty times. Because that's what will help you become winners.'

Luce sat down, leaving the squad a lot happier in their thoughts and raring to get out in the middle against France.

When the bus pulled into the stadium, Ferdia and Joe descended the steps first and both looked around with wonder.

'Imagine, this is one of only two grounds in the world to host the World Cup final in both football and rugby,' said Ferdia. 'And little old you and me are going to be running out on it in an hour or so...'

CHAPTER 47

Kim waited at the head of her team as they lined up in the tunnel for the opening ceremony. They were the third team to be called, between Argentina and Australia.

'Atlantis Rockall' came the announcement over the loudspeakers, and the green and blue tracksuits drew admiring cheers and purrs of approval from the television commentators, even though lots of people all over the world were rushing to their atlases to find this new country on the map. All the other teams were representing countries, although some, like Andorra and Russia, were dedicated rugby academies, or like AtlaRock, an all-round sporting school.

The squad lined up in the centre of the field and waited impatiently for the ceremony to be over. Kim always enjoyed watching these things on television but she now realised how tedious they must be for athletes – especially when they're itching to get on with the action.

When the ceremonies were over, Kim and her team wandered over to their seats and watched Ireland take on Tuvalu in the opening game. All the Atlanteans, plus Ferdia were cheering for Ireland so the rest decided to cheer for the Pacific islanders.

'Come on Tubaloo,' called Sofie, trying to annoy her team-mates, although that was harder to do after Ireland raced into a 21-0 lead at half-time. Kelly signalled the kids to join her down at the tunnel.

'It's almost showtime,' she smiled, as the ten lined up waiting for the first game to finish. 'I want you to relax when you get out there, as all the work has been done and you have lots of plans in your head. Kim will make the calls, but don't be afraid to take any chance that might come your way. We're playing France, so no one in the whole world expects you to win, except maybe me. So, enjoy everything about today, and do your very best.'

And with that, the final whistle blew out on the field and the team representing AtlaRock – as Jess had decided it should be spelled – jogged out across the running track to prepare for action.

Kim glanced across at their opponents, who looked very fit and tanned.

'I bet they weren't fluting around the Arctic Circle for the last two months,' snorted Annie.

'More like the Riviera working on their suntans,' agreed Sofie.

'Bet there weren't too many polar bears down there,' said Ajit. 'At least we know we can run faster than anyone if there's a large scary bear chasing us.'

The referee called the captains together, tossed a coin, and before Kim knew what was happening she was preparing to kick off. Kelly had a variety of moves she had come up with for the kick-offs, which she reckoned were a very important part of Sevens. Kim decided to be adventurous and called '15,' a signal that she wasn't going to kick the ball very high in the air, so her players could sprint towards where she aimed and gather the ball quickly. The move caught out the French, who expected a more obvious high, hanging kick, with the result that Magnus caught the ball unchallenged and was able to feed it back to Rakel without any opponent even coming near them.

Rakel looked up and fired the ball across to Kim, who moved it on to Ferdia, who made a darting move to his left before suddenly stopping and spinning onto his right foot. The switch completely fooled the French centre and Ferdia made for the wide gap which had opened. With a quick burst of speed, he was away racing to touch the ball down under the posts for a stunning try.

The French team were already fighting among themselves, blaming one another for not picking up the runners, with the most blame reserved for the poor centre.

'They haven't touched the ball yet,' laughed Jess, as she ran up to collect it from Ferdia.

Professor Kossuth smiled from the stands as he watched Jess get into position, bounce the ball, pick her spot, and gently drop the ball to the turf. From the moment she kicked it he – and she – knew it was successful. Little Atla-Rock 7 Mighty France 0!

One of the quirky differences about Sevens was that the side who had just scored got to take the kick-off, unlike in 15-a-side rugby. It meant Kim was back into action again and she tried another of the moves from Kelly's playbook. This didn't lead to a try, but the way the AtlaRock defence stayed firm was greatly encouraging. Amazingly, the score was still 7-0 when the half-time whistle blew.

Kelly rushed on with a box full of water bottles, and all the players swigged from them as the coach gave them her views in the brief two-minute interval. She was very positive about the way they were playing and outlined the switches she was going to make, ensuring everyone got a run and no one was flogged too hard in the first game.

The French came at Atlantis hard in the second half and scored a try after a couple of attacks. They dominated for the next couple of minutes but the scores were still level when the Atlantis forwards won a scrum. Magnus picked up the ball and started to run at the French defence, but just as he was tackled he flicked the ball back to Rakel, who had half a second to make a decision as two French backs converged on her.

Recalling the fancy footwork of Deryck St Vincent, she twirled and swivelled on one foot before darting through the gap between the puzzled French players. With only the sweeper to beat, she threw a long pass across to Kim who raced in for the second try. Jess's kick was true, and Kim suddenly realised that they were in a fantastic position to pull off a huge shock.

She urged her team onwards, screaming at them to retain possession from her kick and tearing into every ruck to support her forwards. After what felt like twenty minutes, but was really only two, the referee blew the final whistle. The tournament rules said they had to leave the pitch immediately, but no one begrudged them a half a minute of hugs and wild dancing as they celebrated an amazing victory.

CHAPTER 48

With more than three hours to their next game, the AtlaRock players did their own thing while they waited. Craig, Ferdia and Annie lay down on benches in the changing rooms and fell asleep, Rakel, Ajit, Sofie and Jess decided to explore the stadium, rambling all over the vast complex and meeting people from all over the world. Kim, Joe and Magnus just decided to soak up the atmosphere of the tournament by watching as many matches as they could.

The second game they saw featured their next two opponents, Australia and Russia, so they concentrated hard on their special moves and tactics. The Russians proved to be very physical – one of the Aussies had to be taken off with what looked like a broken rib after just two minutes – and they made their extra height and weight count. They shocked the spectators by taking the lead soon after that and extending it to 12-0 at half-time.

Kim watched as the Australian coach almost exploded at half-time, so angry was he at his team's performance. The team responded with a well-prepared move for a try just after the break, but the Russians had also been doing their homework and kept working away at the weakness of the sweeper under a high ball.

It paid off when the unfortunate defender spilled the ball under his posts and the Russian hooker sprinted through to pick up the loose ball and score.

'17 points to 7, Russia leads with ten seconds left,' came the stadium announcer's voice as she began the countdown to full-time. And just as the crowd hailed the giant-killing acts of Atlantis-Rockall, so did they cheer to the rafters the victory of the Russians over Australia.

'Well that's thrown our group wide open,' said Joe with a grin. 'The Aussies will be coming at us hard after that.'

'They're very beatable,' replied Kim. 'We can do the same to them. I'm not sure we can beat the Russians though, they're enormous, and rough.'

'We beat those Brazilians, though,' Joe reminded her. 'And they were all huge.'

Outside, on one of the practice pitches, Ajit was having a bit of fun with some Japanese kids. He had brought his hurley along with him and was practicing some long-distance pucks when three of the locals started running to try and catch the ball before it landed. They even made a game of it, taking it in turns to catch it in their right hand and in their left, and trying to fire the ball back so Ajit would hit it back on the volley.

'I think you've just invented Japanese Cricket,' said Jess, as they all joined in with the fun.

As the morning session went on, the players began to drift back to the players area of the grandstand to join Kim.

'You should get up and check out the rest of the stadium, Kim,' bubbled Sofie. 'It's an amazing place. And so many people have come to watch, too.'

Kim smiled and looked around the ground, pinching herself to check she wasn't dreaming.

'Right,' she announced, 'everyone's here now, let's go down and get ready for these Aussies.'

Kelly talked to the players about what she had seen in the Australians' game against Russia, and Kim chipped in with a few comments too. They both expected their opponents to drop the sweeper who had made the mistake in their first game and they were proved correct.

The Aussies were very determined to repair the damage

done to their chances and played cautiously at first. When Magnus tackled their scrum-half too high they opted to kick the penalty and took a 3-0 lead. From the kick-off, the ball was knocked on by the Aussie prop and Jess pounced on the loose ball, speeding diagonally across the field and diving over in the corner. She bounced up quickly – pausing briefly to thank Professor Olsen in her mind – and shaped to take the conversion. It was a tricky angle, but she hit the ball well and it crept in close to the left-hand upright.

The Aussies hit back immediately, their very speedy winger taking advantage of Kim snoozing for a second and once she was past the defenders there was no way she could be caught. Kim apologised to her teammates but told them to forget it and stay focused on their plan. But another slip, this time by Ferdia, saw the same winger run in another try and at the interval Australia were 17-7 ahead.

CHAPTER 49

Kelly told the Atlanteans not to panic, that there were ways through the Australian defence, and as long as they kept the ball away from their speedy wing they had a great chance. Unfortunately, Jess was penalised almost from the kick-off and their opponents took the three points.

Kim ran her eye across the Australian defence – they had made some changes at the break and that unfortunate defender was now on the field, looking more nervous than ever before. Kim felt a little sorry for him but realised there was no room for sympathy when it came to winning the game. She would give him a hug after the final whistle but while the game was on they would look to exploit the Australians' weakest link.

She noticed he was so wary of getting involved that he backed away and pointed to the player next to him when his team-mates were looking to pass to someone. But the trouble with having just seven players on the field is that there is nowhere to hide.

There isn't nearly as much kicking from open play in Sevens Rugby, but Kim decided to test the nervous player playing at sweeper, so she launched the ball high into the air.

She raced to follow the ball as it descended, keeping her eye on the sweeper as she got closer. He backed away as he saw her getting nearer to him, allowing her the space to leap and snatch the ball before it hit the ground. Her momentum carried her through the defender and she landed with her hands stretched out and the ball grounded behind the line.

'Prrrrrreeeeep!' sounded the referee's whistle, as she signalled a try under the posts for Atlantis-Rockall. Jess duly added the conversion to leave her side six points down with two minutes left to play.

Kim got to kick off again and signalled the '15' move again that had worked so well against France.

Magnus took the ball and went on a run, breaking through the arms of the winger who, although fast, was no tackler. He was close to the touchline so he decided to start veering inside to improve the angle for Jess. The sweeper came rushing towards him but he sidestepped him easily and with a skip crossed the line to score.

Magnus was swamped by the rest of his squad, but Jess quickly snatched the ball from his grasp and pointed out the countdown clock which showed 12 seconds had already passed since his try. She gathered her thoughts, bounced the ball as the professor had shown her, and dropped it towards her foot. There was a moment of pure silence in the stadium as every spectator focused on Jess's right boot, followed by a huge cheer as the ball flew hard and high into the air and crossed the crossbar between the posts.

It was Jess's turn to be swamped as the other nine kids showed their delight at her dramatic kick. The referee ushered them to the middle to restart but the hooter sounded before Kim could kick the ball so she hoofed it into the crowd and raced off to celebrate on the running track alongside.

'Yippee!' exclaimed Kelly as she greeted the players. 'That was fantastic – and we're almost certainly into the quarter-finals! We definitely will be if we beat Russia.'

That last bit didn't sound too easy, thought Kim, but she went along with Kelly's delight as she didn't want to poop the party.

'Let's go and watch the Russians and see if we can spot

any weaknesses,' the coach suggested and all the team joined her in the stand this time. The French matched the Russians for power but they made some stupid mistakes and went down by a scoreline of 35-26.

Ferdia checked the scoreboard, and started scribbling in the tournament programme before he stood up to address the team.

'I've checked it twice, and I think we've qualified already for the quarters,' he said.

'Of course we have,' said Kim. 'Did you really need a pen and paper to work out that Russia and us have both won two out of two, and France and Australia have lost two out of two. They can't catch either of us!'

'That makes the last game this evening what they call a dead rubber,' said Kelly, 'but it's still important in deciding who you play from now on. We'll probably get an easier opponent in the quarters if we beat Russia.'

CHAPTER 50

By the time the last game of day one came around all the players from the big teams had crammed into the fenced-off players' viewing area to watch the two surprise packets of the tournament that had knocked out two of rugby's superpowers – the enormous country that spanned two continents, and the two tiny rocks.

The television reporters were much more interested in talking to the Atlantis-Rockall players than they had been earlier, so Luce gave Kim a bit of coaching in what to say to them. But after a while Kim got fed up answering all the boring questions with boring answers such as 'We're just delighted to be here and we'll do our very best to make everyone proud of us back home.'

She was glad when she got back to her team and they could start planning the downfall of Russia. Kelly gave them her usual detailed team-talk, and Luce asked Kalvin to say a few words to inspire them.

'I'm not very good at this sort of thing,' he started. 'But I know you're a great bunch of kids, and I've been impressed with how well you all get on together. Throwing you into a cramped submarine was a big test, and you've passed. You're not ten players from Ireland, Greenland, Scotland, or wherever. You're a team,' he added, to the cheers of the kids.

They were just preparing to march out to face Russia when Rakel screamed.

'What is it?' asked Kim, as she rushed over to where her friend was sitting. Luce had let Rakel keep the Russian mobile phone in case the kidnappers got in touch, and she was holding it in her hand.

'Look,' the youngster cried, 'look! They're hurting her!'

Kim stared at the screen, which showed Rakel's mother standing in a forest glade, beside a stream. Her mouth was gagged and her eyes bandaged so she could not speak or see anything. Kim took the phone from Rakel and passed it to Luce whose face turned white.

And just at that moment the referee stuck her head around the door to say play would begin in four minutes. After she'd left Craig asked Rakel was she OK to play, but the youngster just burst into tears.

'It's OK, Rak,' said Kim. 'We'll be fine. The game isn't

important anyway, because we've already qualified.'

'Kim's right,' said Luce. 'You just stay here with me and we'll get in touch with the police in the Faroes.

'Good luck Kim,' the Atlantis manager nodded, signalling that it was time to leave the dressing room.

Out on the field Kim found it hard to get Rakel's mum out of her head, but the impending rugby match had her worried too. It was hard enough playing with one player missing, but it was only up close she noticed how big their opponents were.

'Aren't we playing in an Under 13 competition?' asked Annie.

'Yes….' said Kim.

'Well that fella over there has stubble on his face,' she replied, pointing at the Russian prop.

Kim winced. 'Nothing we can do, Annie, let's just focus on the game.'

'What's the story with scrum-half, Kelly?' asked Joe. 'It looks like Rakel won't be playing today.'

Kelly frowned. 'That's a problem. Will we switch Jess back?'

'Oh, please don't,' said Jess, 'I much prefer it on the wing and I get to run more.'

'I agree,' said Kelly, 'you're a greater asset as winger.'

'What about Ajit,' suggested Joe. 'He's been talking about wanting to play there for ages and he'd be perfect for the role.'

'Great idea,' said Kim. 'Don't worry about the calls and the plays Kelly, I'll be beside him for all that.'

Kelly nodded. 'I'll leave you to it,' she smiled. 'Good luck!'

Ajit was a bit stunned when his new role was explained to him, but he said he was game for it so they all moved into their positions and waited for the Russian out-half to kick off.

CHAPTER 51

That they lost the game was no fault of Ajit's. Or anyone, really. The Russians were just too big, strong and ruthless for the Atlantis-Rockall side.

Besides that, they also appeared to know in advance all the moves that Kim was calling. She even renamed a few calls during the half-time huddle, but to no avail.

'They knew everything we were going to do,' sighed Kim in the dressing room after the game. 'Not just the Rakel stuff, or the cameraman on those islands, but stuff like our calls. They must have had a spy in among those Japanese schoolkids all week.'

Kelly looked very angry. 'You're right Kim, and it's terrible that a coach would do such a thing – especially with a team of kids.'

'Some of them are very big and hairy kids,' complained Ferdia.

'I know, I know,' replied Kelly, 'but you'll just have to forget that. With a bit of luck, we won't have to face them again as they're in the other half of the draw in the quarter-finals. England will hammer them.'

'Oh, yes, I nearly forgot we were in the quarters,' said Joe. 'Who are we playing tomorrow?'

'You better sit down before I tell you Joe,' joked Kelly. 'And Ferdia, Ajit, Kim, Craig and Jess, too…'

'Not Ireland,' screamed Craig. 'How are we supposed to play against our own country?'

'Ireland's not your country when you're here,' said Magnus. 'When you're in the World Cup you're an Atlantean, an Atla-Rocker.'

'Well said Magnus,' said Kelly. 'We are indeed playing Ireland, but they are just one more opponent we have to beat. And we'll have a plan for that later on this evening. Now, the bus is outside, get yourselves on board, we're moving to Tokyo and I'll see you all in the hotel for dinner.'

Rakel was sitting in an armchair in the lobby talking to Luce when the team walked into their new hotel. She was still upset but brightened up when she saw her friends.

'I heard the result, I'm so sorry,' she told Kim.

'That wasn't your fault and I don't think you would have made any difference. They are a lot bigger than us. Ajit did well, to be fair.'

Rakel looked at the carpet. 'I hope you forgive me missing today. If it's OK I think I'll be right to play tomorrow – as a sub, of course.'

Kim smiled. 'That's great, and don't worry Rak, he didn't do that well. I'll talk to Kelly – but she'll pick the team.'

The squad were still buzzing that night. Their amazing success was all over the TV news and other hotel guests kept coming up to them to congratulate them and ask them for selfies or autographs. They retreated to the team room but the hotel staff called in to tell them whenever they cropped up on the television.

Kim looked around the room where Craig looked like his head was about to explode – although he didn't know how to read Japanese he had bought a Manga comic reckoning he could understand what was going on from the pictures. That may have been the case, but he didn't realise Japanese people read a book from the back page and move from right to left, the opposite to Western readers. It was all too much for Craig who flung the book across the room in frustration, knocking over the Yugioh card game that Annie and Ajit were enjoying.

The rest of the team were chatting, or trying to understand what was going on in the TV shows, so Kim slipped quietly away to bed.

CHAPTER 52

Kim wasn't asleep when Rakel came to bed an hour or so later, but she pretended she was. She had been struggling to sleep as her mind tossed over the events of the day. She was joyful about the amazing wins over France and Australia, nervous about the rest of the tournament, and very worried indeed about Rakel and her mother. Talking to Rakel wouldn't make it any easier to doze off.

She was awoken by a cry.

'Are you all right Rak?' she answered.

'Yes... I suppose,' Rakel replied.

'What's up with that cry?' asked Kim.

'I... I just had an idea,' said Rakel. 'I had a dream about one of our school outings last year... it was to a place called Vioarlundin Park.

'The thing about the Faroes is, we have very few trees on the islands – it's too windy and too salty is the reason they taught us in school. But one of the few places they do grow is Vioarlundin, a park in the capital, Torshavn.'

Kim looked puzzled.

'But don't you see?' asked Rakel. 'That photo of mum showed her in a forest. If they're still in the Faroes then they must be in Vioarlundin!'

Kim sat up straight in bed. 'What time is it there now? It's... 5am here,' she said, checking the bedside clock.

'Then it's about nine o'clock last night there,' replied Rakel. 'That's still early enough to ring the cops, I think.'

'Yes... but is it too early to wake up Luce?' said Kim, with a frown.

Surprisingly, Luce didn't seem to mind being disturbed.

'I couldn't sleep either,' she said when she answered the door. 'Do come in.'

Rakel explained her idea about the forest, and Luce appeared interested at first.

'But surely they would have worked that out themselves,' she suggested.

'They should have,' said Rakel, 'but our police are not used to such crimes.'

'It's late on Saturday night there,' said Luce, 'they mightn't answer the phone.'

'Please Luce, I can't bear to think of my mum out there in

the park at night, it's very cold in my country,' replied Rakel.

Kim asked Luce could she speak to her alone, and she signalled to follow her out into the corridor.

'Luce, if you leave it till the morning to ring the police then the tournament will be over,' said Kim, whispering urgently. 'The rugby isn't that important compared to her mum's safety but we need Rakel to play for us and she will be in no state to do that when she's still missing.'

Luce nodded in reply and walked back into her hotel room.

'All right, you two need to get to bed and try to sleep – you will both need your energy today. I'm going to ring the Faroes police right now and hopefully we'll have good news by the time you wake up.'

But there was no good news from Luce when she got downstairs and met them in the breakfast room.

'Their phones just rang out. There was no answer,' she said, apologising to Rakel, who started to cry.

Magnus came upon the trio and asked what was happening.

'Can you give me your phone please Luce?' he asked after hearing the explanation. 'I may be able to help.'

Magnus dialled a number and walked away a short distance. He had a brief conversation on the phone before returning to the table, handing the mobile back to Luce.

'Thank you, Luce. I rang my dad there – he's a great friend of the prime minister from their days ocean rowing. I asked him to get his pal to give the cops a kick in the butt.'

Kim and Rakel smiled. 'Well I suppose that might work – it's certainly worth trying. Thank you,' said Rakel.

CHAPTER 53

The Ireland players were surprised to hear so many Irish accents lined up *against* them before their quarter-final match in Tokyo.

'I thought you guys were all Greek, or Eskimos, if that's even a word,' said Ross, the Ireland out-half. 'What club do you play rugby with anyway?'

Kim told him the name of her school, and then explained that none of the rest of them had ever played a proper game of rugby before yesterday, but that they had the best coaches in the world.

Ross turned white.

From the kick-off the Atlanteans went on the attack, and after a lovely sidestep by Kim the ball went to Jess who spotted a gap in the Irish defence. She veered towards the touchline and remembered one of the things Oddy had taught her, leaning on the edge of her boot and spinning out of the grasp of the onrushing tackler.

It left her free to race all the way to the posts and touch

down for the opening try.

Kim tried a similar move from the following kick-off but this time she switched the direction of the attack and returned the ball to Magnus and Ajit, who swapped passes twice to reach the try-line before Magnus bundled over it for the score. Jess missed the kick but a 12-0 lead for Atla-Rock had stunned the Ireland team, and the crowd.

'Come on Ireland,' called Ross. 'This is not acceptable.'

Kim smiled, and ran back to prepare to kick off once again. The Ireland players were starting to panic, and the next time Jess got the ball two players rushed to tackle her. One of them caught her around the shoulders, and the referee signalled a penalty for a high tackle. Jess remained on the ground however, just lifting her hand to call for assistance.

'It really hurts Kim,' she said, when the captain arrived at her side. 'I might have broken a rib.'

Kim called for the medical staff and rushed over to Kelly to let her know what was happening.

'Get Craig on,' said Kim, 'he's our best cover for the backs and I'm not sure Rakel is up to it yet.'

The paramedics helped Jess off and the referee signalled

to Kim that they had a penalty to take.

'Oh no, Jess is our kicker,' she said.

'You're not bad yourself,' said Magnus. 'Now hurry up or you'll run out of time.'

The referee pointed at his watch and opened his hand twice to signal there were just ten seconds left to take the penalty. Kim bounced the ball and steadied herself, as she had seen Jess do so many times, and let the ball fall just as she swung her leg back. It connected well, and although she didn't get the satisfying sight of seeing the ball soar high between the posts, her kick had enough distance to clear the crossbar. The sight of the two officials raising their flags was satisfying enough for Kim.

'Fifteen-nil!' said Ajit.

'We won't be able to go home if we keep this up,' said Joe with a wide grin.

That remained the score until the two-minute break, when Kelly rushed on for a quick team talk.

'Jess isn't too bad, it seems – there's no break, they say, but she's going to have some bruising and will need to be strapped up. She won't be right to play today though.'

Kim noticed a few of the players frowning, so she moved

in quickly to stop that.

'That's unfortunate for Jess,' she said, 'but we'll be fine. Craig has already shown he has the pace and skill to be a great winger and we just need to get the ball to him and he'll finish the job.'

Craig smiled, and sure enough, the confidence boost was just what he needed. The first time he received a pass he took off at speed, sidestepping and darting in and out like an Olympic speed skater. He rounded the Irish sweeper with ease and fell to the ground for AtlaRock's third try.

The score – which brought the lead to 22 points and meant Ireland would need to score four times in five minutes to win – took the wind out of their opponents' sails and the rest of the game was barely contested by either side.

'You didn't seem to have much problem with scoring against Ireland, Craig,' Magnus told him as they walked off. Craig looked at him, and they exchanged huge grins and high fives.

In the other quarter-finals, England beat Scotland and Russia beat Fiji, who had been one of the tournament favourites, but the Atlantis-Rockall kids stayed around mostly to watch the last of the games, as they would be playing the winners next. Japan were brave, but despite huge support from the Tokyo crowd, they were no match for New Zealand.

'We're playing the All Blacks! Wow,' said Kim. 'Their men and women are the best in the world. Their kids look pretty good too, don't they?'

'We look pretty good too,' said Magnus. 'Let's see how it goes.'

CHAPTER 54

The New Zealanders were very well drilled, but Kelly was secretly very happy to be playing them. She had spent a lot of the voyage watching their games in the South Pacific Schools Championship and had studied their moves very closely. She had watched all their games in Yokohama too and reckoned she had spotted some flaws in their line-up, which she shared with her team.

'We're playing them in less than two hours,' said Kelly, 'so stay close to the dressing room as we will run through a few moves before the game.'

Kim and Rakel wandered off to have look at the stadium while the games to decide 9th to 16th places were being played. The arena was brand new, with seats for 80,000 people. The ground had been full until Japan lost to New Zealand, after which almost half the crowd left, but there was still a scary amount of people watching the tournament.

The AtlaRock girls struggled to walk too far without being stopped for selfies, and soon grew tired of trying to.

As they made their way back towards the dressing room, Rakel suddenly froze, and ducked in behind a pillar.

'What's up?' asked Kim.

Rakel pointed over her shoulder at a tall man with dark hair leaning up against the wall outside the players' area.

'That's the guy from the bookshop,' she gasped.

Kim joined her behind the pillar and studied the man. He was obviously waiting for someone as he kept looking for his watch and looking towards the door.

'Let's wait a few minutes,' suggested Kim, 'I'd love to know what he's doing here.'

They remained behind the pillar until the man was approached by a woman in a tracksuit. He stood up straight and shook her hand, and she showed him into the players' area.

'That's one of the coaches!' said Kim.

'Yes, and did you see the colour of her tracksuit? It was red, white and blue – I suppose she could be French, but I'd be willing to bet my favourite cat that she's with the Russian team.'

Kim and Rakel followed the adults through the doorway to the area reserved for the participating teams. The older pair had disappeared into one of the rooms off the corridor, so the AtlaRock players decided to head back to their dressing room.

Luce was there, chatting with Kalvin and Kelly, and the kids filled her in on what they had seen. Luce jumped up out of her seat and rushed into a room off the main changing area. On her return she handed the phone to Rakel.

'Tell this man what you saw, both in the bookshop and here, just now. He wants you to describe the man you saw as well as you can. You too, Kim.'

The kids explained as best they could to the policeman, who was Japanese. He said he'd need to talk to them at the end of the day and would call out to the stadium to see them.

'What's happening in Torshavn?' asked Rakel. 'Have they found mum yet?'

'I haven't heard anything yet,' replied Luce. 'But Magnus's call seemed to do the trick to get them moving. I got a call from the Faroes Police at about one o'clock in the morning their time. I don't think they had ever got a phone call at home from their prime minister before!'

The All Blacks started strongly and ran in a soft try in the first minute of the game.

'That's terrible defending there, Atlantis,' said Kim, 'let's make sure that doesn't happen again. Now, Magnus, when they kick off I want you chasing hard to attack the ball. We have to get it back to start working on a score – let's try the move down the channel Kelly suggested.'

The Kiwi out-half missed his kick – and was so rattled by it that he mistimed his drop kick on kick-off. It flew straight into the arms of Magnus, who made about ten metres before he turned and fed the ball back to Ajit.

Ajit moved to make a pass out to Kim, but instead of releasing the ball he spun around on his toes and slipped into the gap between two players in black shirts. He raced away, touching down under the posts and flipping the ball back to his captain to complete the conversion.

The crowd bellowed their approval, and the All Blacks suddenly looked very worried indeed. Any fancy move they tried there was an Atlantean or Rockaller there to counter it, and their frustration led to mistakes, one of which saw Craig collect a knock-on and, with the referee allowing him advantage, flew down the wing to score a try in the corner.

The angle made the kick too difficult for Kim, but the 12-5 lead put a huge grin on Kelly's face at half-time.

'That was fantastic, kids,' she gasped. 'You're doing everything right. Just keep that up and you'll win this. They're really rattled.'

Kelly's plans kept AtlaRock in the game all the way up to the final minute, when Ajit was caught in two minds between a pass and a run, and he was nailed by the All Blacks prop. The ball squirted towards their out-half who collected and set off on an angled run across the field. Craig and Annie chased him hard and forced him into the corner, but their efforts weren't enough to stop him scoring.

The clock was already in the red zone, so the Kiwi kicker had to make the conversion to level the scores. The Atla-Rock players lined up nervously beside the posts, but Ferdia already had a broad grin on his face.

As the ball soared towards the goal, Ferdia threw his hands up in the air. The touch judges also raised their arms to signal the ball was over the bar.

'What are you doing, you eejit?' asked Joe. 'It's a draw, we've got to play extra time.'

'Read the regulations, kids!' laughed Ferdia. 'There's no

extra time. In the case of a draw, it goes on tries scored, and as that was also level at two each, the winner is whoever scored the first try. Thanks to Ajit, we had already won!'

CHAPTER 55

The referee nodded that Ferdia was right, and the rest of the team joined in with the celebrations.

'World Cup final, can you believe it?' said Craig.

'At a sport I hadn't even heard of two months ago,' laughed Sofie.

Jess and Rakel raced out to join them, but the tournament officials quickly ushered them off the field to allow the second semi-final to take place.

'What time is the final?' Kim asked Luce.

'Well it's fixed for just under two hours after the finish of the second semi-final. They'll play all the plate and other competitions semis and finals, and the third-place play-off before the Grand Final. I suggest you all get some rest and relax back in the changing room. Stay and watch this game and I'll organise some food and drink for you,' she said, as she disappeared down the tunnel.

The AtlaRockers found their seats and watched as England took on Russia in what looked like a game between two under 18 sides rather than under 13s.

'They're so big,' complained Sofie as the two front rows collided for the first scrum. Magnus, Joe and Ferdia looked at each other nervously.

The game was actually decided after just three minutes play, when the English out-half was crushed by a very late tackle by the giant Russian prop. The player had to be taken off on a stretcher as she held her ribs and bit her lip. The prop was given a yellow-card, but that meant he was off the field for just two minutes, his unfortunate victim would be out for the rest of the tournament.

The English players seemed to lose their nerve every time they got the ball when either of the props was anywhere nearby, and the Russian pressure began to tell on the scoreboard. They took the lead just before the break and ran in three more tries after it to win 26-0.

If they had any doubts before, Atlantis-Rockall knew they had an enormous job to win the cup now.

Down in the changing room, no one wanted to talk about the game. Some of the players seemed content with getting as far as they had, and that they would always be able to tell their friends about the day they played in a World Cup final.

Kim didn't see it like that and so gathered the players around her while the adults were off doing other things.

'Don't look at getting to the final as the achievement, the real prize is that golden trophy out there,' she told the squad. 'Getting to the final just gives us a shot at it, which is more than the English, and French, and New Zealanders will have. We'll probably never have a shot at a game like this in the rest of our lives.

'I don't want to remember today as a game we never believed we could win, and we surrendered before we even went out there. Kelly is a fantastic coach and she has guided us all the way here. The stuff we learned from Oddy, and Professor Kossuth, have all been incredibly useful too.

'These people believed in us, and we can't let them down by not trying our utmost to win this. I believe in you too.'

Kim sat down, and after a couple of seconds of stunned silence Magnus started to clap, and everyone joined in.

'Good on you, Kim,' said Ferdia, 'that was powerful.'

Kim smiled, and Rakel gave her a hug. 'Thanks Kim, you're the greatest captain in the world.'

At that moment, Luce came rushing into the room.

'Rakel, we have some news for you,' she announced, thrusting the kidnappers' mobile phone at her.

Rakel stared at the screen, but where there had previously been a gagged and bound photo of her mother crying, now there was a live video of her smiling and crying tears of joy.

'Rakel, Rakel,' she cried, before telling her daughter in Faroese that she was safe, well and so grateful that she and her friends had helped rescue her.

Rakel took the phone into the side room for a private chat but returned soon afterwards with a broad beam on her face. Kim had never seen her so happy.

'It was very dramatic,' she said. 'After Magnus woke up the prime minister, and he woke up the police, they went to the spot I told them I recognised. They found some footprints that led them to the shack they were keeping my mum. The cops went in with their guns pointed and the Russian agents surrendered.'

'Wow, your poor mum, but she must be delighted to be free,' said Annie.

'They're taking her home now, but she told me the cops have seized a computer and the kidnappers' phones. They've sent the data off them over to the Japanese policeman who is investigating that guy who was in the bookshop.'

'That's fantastic news,' said Kelly, 'now, how are you fixed to play in a World Cup final?'

CHAPTER 56

Ajit had earlier confided to Kelly that he had strained a muscle in his calf and he didn't think he would be able to start. He agreed to get some physio and to line out as a substitute in case one was needed.

Kelly had been racking her brain trying to work out her options – including debating whether she should try to convince Rakel to play – when the youngster suddenly had that huge weight lifted from her shoulders.

'I'd love to play,' said Rakel, 'but what about Aj?'

'I'm not 100 per cent,' he replied. 'I'd much prefer if you started too.'

Kelly sat down and told them who would be the starting seven, and what her plans were to counteract the power and aggression of the Russians. She had spent hours going through the videos of their games in Yokohama the night before. When she was finished speaking the students were much more confident about their chances.

'What I don't understand is why they would go to such

lengths to cheat in a competition that's only for kids after all,' said Joe.

Kim sighed. 'I know, and I can't imagine caring so much that I would hurt people to cheat others out of a trophy.'

Luce sat down and smiled. 'We haven't got to this in your History of Sport course, but a very great novelist wrote something about sport that I often quote to my classes. He said, "Serious sport has nothing to do with fair play. It is bound up with hatred, jealousy, boastfulness, disregard of all rules and pleasure in witnessing violence. In other words, it is war minus the shooting."

'That's why the people behind the Russian team have taken winning this competition so seriously. We don't know who they are – they could be wealthy individuals or companies who are willing to do almost anything to win this 'war.' They could be acting on behalf of some arm of the state. But they want to win at all costs and that's what we are so opposed to on Atlantis. Sport will always be about good things like friendship, team spirit and having respect for your opponent, win or lose.'

The AtlaRock team finished their preparations and their

warm-up. Luce produced special shirts she had made up with gold embroidery under the crest, saying 'World Cup final' and the date of the game. She shook each player's hand as she presented them with a shirt and wished them luck.

When they were ready to leave, they players lined up behind Kim. Even Jess was togged out, strapped up and ready to play if she were needed.

They walked out, side by side with the Russians, and were stunned to see the stadium was packed once more. The organisers had allowed anyone who wanted to see the final to come in free and the 80,000 crowd was an amazing sight for the players.

As they reached the middle, and lined up to meet the VIP guests, Kim's eye was caught by the arrival of about twenty Japanese policemen on the sideline. They rushed over to the Russian bench and grabbed the woman coach they had seen outside earlier. Kim and Rakel also noticed that there were policemen also standing beside a tall man in a dark suit, and they were holding his arms tightly behind his back as they put on handcuffs.

'What's going on there?' asked Kim.

'That's the bookshop guy,' said Rakel. 'And the Japanese

cop who was dealing with the kidnap is talking to him.'

Not only was the policeman talking to the agent, he was turning out his pockets too.

'OK, team, take your eyes off what's happening over there and let's focus on what we're about to do on the pitch,' said Kim, although she found it hard to avert her gaze herself.

The VIPs were also distracted, but not nearly as much as the Russian team. Once the ceremony was over the red carpet was rolled up and the teams lined up ready to receive Kim's kick-off.

But just as she was taking aim at where she wanted Magnus to be, the referee blew several blasts on her whistle.

'What is going on,' she shouted, as four uniformed police-men, a detective and the tournament's chief organiser came running on to the pitch.

The organiser and the detective walked up to the referee.

'I apologise for this incursion,' the rugby man said. 'We have just discovered from the police that at least two of the players here have been playing with falsified documents. A computer was seized last night in the Faroe Islands which appeared to show that two of the Russian players are five years older than their passports say they are. We were trying to verify this information when the police arrested that gentleman over there,' he added, pointing at the bookshop spy.

'He was carrying their real passports, which prove that the two props are actually eighteen years of age. They have been expelled from the tournament.'

CHAPTER 57

The Russian props were led away by police without a word, but their captain was very angry.

'What is happening here,' he complained. 'We cannot play without Sergei and Oleg. And our coach has been arrested too, and our manager. This is unfair, we demand that you award us the tournament as we have already beaten this pathetic little team of tiny islands. We refuse to play.'

The tournament organiser listened, and smiled.

'Listen, sir,' he began, 'there are eighty thousand people here, and hundreds of millions watching on television and the internet. They want to see a Grand Final, which is the only reason why we haven't asked the police to arrest your whole team. We are having a meeting tonight which may decide to ban not just the Moscow Rugby Academy, but all of Russia from every rugby tournament for the next ten years, and all you players from any international competition.

'I could recommend that we let off the players, as you may have been unaware of what your officials were up to. But if you don't play this final, then that will not be possible. Perhaps you could explain that to your country's President. I'm sure he would be very understanding.'

And with that he left the field. The referee turned to the Russian captain.

'Do you want to play?' he asked.

'We'll play,' snarled the youth, who turned to Kim. 'And we will demolish your little team with the winds of fury.'

Kim smiled and jogged back to her team to let them know what was going on.

'The game's going ahead, but those two monster props won't be troubling us this time. Their coach is gone too. But be careful, they're angry, especially that captain lad.'

When the game eventually kicked off the Russians appeared very rattled and disorganised. The two players who replaced Sergei and Oleg in the front row were barely half their size, and were not used to playing in the forwards.

Magnus went on a couple of rampaging runs, switching passes with Joe as they made their way upfield. Joe controlled the ball in a ruck just outside the Russian twenty-two and spotted Craig starting to accelerate, he flung the ball out as far as he could to his right and it landed perfectly, just in front of Craig who gathered and raced through the open field to score at the posts.

Kim added the conversion, and noticed the Russians were fighting among themselves. She watched as the captain pushed over the scrum-half and screamed at the bench for their only remaining replacement to come on.

'This is very messy,' said Joe.

'I know,' said Kim, 'but we must keep our concentration. They still have some dangerous players, especially that out-half.'

Kim was proved right with the next play, with the captain rushing to dispossess Magnus from the kick-off and feeding his powerful running backs. Craig made good ground but was unable to catch them and the scores were soon level.

The Japanese crowd, who didn't understand what had happened before the game, were starting to feel sorry for the understrength Russians, and their try got as big a cheer as AtlaRock's.

'What are that crowd like,' sniffed Annie. 'I thought neutrals always cheered for the underdog. The biggest country in the world against two postage stamps and they cheer for *them*?'

The final was played over ten minutes a side, but the score remained at 7-7 when the interval arrived.

Kelly came on to point out a few things they might do better, and as she was leaving she whispered to Kim that she might bring on Jess if they needed a score with five minutes left.

'I had the doctor check the x-rays and he's had another look at her. She's fine, just a little sore.'

'Great,' said Kim. 'It could be useful to have her extra pace.'

Again, Kim was proved right. The Russians used the interval to gather their thoughts and they reorganised themselves. They came out hard after the break and one of their replacement props scored another try out wide, which wasn't converted.

Both sides exchanged breakaway tries, Craig doing the honours for Atlantis-Rockall, but the Russians still had a five-point advantage with four minutes remaining. Kim looked across at the bench and opened her hands wide in front of her to signal to Kelly that they needed to bring on the little speedster.

Jess jogged on, but Kim immediately wondered had she

made a mistake. Every time Jess landed her foot as she ran, she winced. One heavy tackle could do her serious injury.

Kim worried that the Russians might notice, and target Jess, so she decided to keep the ball away from her for as long as she could.

Russia had suddenly realised they had a chance to win the cup and changed their tactics from aggressive attack to resolute defence. They showed no interest in making their way up field, and every time they got the ball they buried it in a ruck to waste time.

Magnus, Joe and Ferdia fought fearlessly to get the ball back, and in the end Joe was successful, feeding it back to Rakel who passed out to Kim.

The out-half knew there were only seconds left, so she momentarily paused to check where Jess and Craig were. The substitute had no one within ten metres of her, so she put her faith in her speed and kick the ball over the Russian heads, and watched it bounce towards the corner. The defenders turned and chased after it, but they hadn't reckoned on the green and blue blur that was speeding down the wing. It briefly stopped to pick up the ball before racing towards the line.

Jess noticed that she was about to be sandwiched between two enormous Russians and remembered something Professor Oddy Olsen had taught her. Just as she reached the line, she stopped in an instant, and spun sideways through the air. The Russian pair collided and Jess fell over, touching the ball down just in time.

There was another enormous cheer – perhaps the crowd just liked watching exciting action and didn't care who won, thought Annie – as the referee signalled the try. Kim looked at the scoreboard which showed the teams were level at 19-19, meaning her conversion could win it. The scoreboard also told her than time was up, and she had just a few seconds to take her kick.

'Sorry Kim, I couldn't get under the posts,' said Jess, but Kim brushed away her apology.

It wasn't an easy kick, but Kim went through everything Professor Kossuth had taught her. She bounced the ball again, gauged the timing of her kick, and dropped it. Her right leg swung back and then forward, connecting perfectly with the ball and sending it straight between the posts.

Kim only had a couple of seconds to enjoy it before she found herself buried by a joyful ruck of team-mates. 'Careful, don't make Jess's ribs any worse,' she called out, but after a few minutes of hugging and laughter they were called over to meet the VIPs once again.

The tournament organiser made short speech in Japanese, and repeated it in English, saying the best team had won, the team that best showed the spirit of sport and international friendship. A woman who someone said was a princess presented Kim with the trophy, and after they had all collected their medals they did a lap of honour around the track.

'This is the greatest day of my life,' roared Craig, 'I just love being adored!'

The rest of his team laughed at him, and took turns to carry the World Cup and show it off to the crowd.

Joe just stared at his medal. 'Isn't it beautiful,' he told Magnus. 'I'll never be parted from this. I'll carry it everywhere to show all my friends and to remind me of a great day.'

Magnus took his medal out of his pocket and jogged over to the edge of the track, where a kid was sitting in a wheelchair. He gave him his baseball cap, and a hug, and just as he was turning to rejoin his friends he ran back and handed the youngster his medal.

'What have you done you lunatic,' said Joe.

'Ah look, it's only a piece of metal,' replied Magnus. 'I'll always remember this day, and I don't need that to remind me of our great victory and the great people I played with. That lad cheered for us all day and when I looked over at him just before Kim took that last kick he gave me a cool thumbs up. He has a nice souvenir now.'

CHAPTER 58

Back on Atlantis, the kids were having fun in the canteen. Craig was telling stupid jokes to try and make Jess laugh, so she could hurt her sides.

They were all allowed a rare opportunity to talk to their families and friends via the internet but nobody complained that Rakel went first and hogged the computer for almost an hour. She told them that they were now national heroes in the Faroe Islands, not just for their help in freeing her mother, but also because of their win in Tokyo.

'They showed the final live on national television, would you believe,' she laughed. 'No one in the whole country had a clue what was going on, but they were all delighted we won.'

Kim had a few minutes chat with her own parents, and she was most thrilled by the expression on her dad's face – the biggest smile she had ever seen there. 'We're so proud of you Kim,' he said, 'even your brother was crying when you put that last kick over.'

Luce and Kalvin arrived, following by all the coaching staff carrying a giant rugby ball-shaped cake.

'This isn't strictly on the nutrition plan we gave you, but this has been a very special day,' said Luce. 'And as it's also my birthday I get to blow out all the candles,' she announced, lighting just one giant candle in the middle of the cake.

'It's been a long dangerous journey from Rockall to here, and I must confess I didn't really expect you to win the competition. But you have an amazing coach, and an amazing captain, and that's half the battle. Atlantis will sail on, and we will have to drop some of you back to Rockall, but I hope you all remember this one fantastic day when you were champions of the world.'

There was a little murmur and a few sad faces when Luce mentioned splitting up the group, but she smiled.

'Oh, I forgot to mention that the owner of Atlantis, Victor, has been very busy lately and he hasn't been able to join us on this adventure. But he did record a little message on the computer which he asked me to play for you.'

Luce pressed a key and the screen sprang to life with Victor's smiling face.

'Thank you, thank you, thank you,' he said, beaming. 'I apologise for not being with you but I watched every minute of the final today. I am so proud of you all, and am delighted to see how well the students of Rockall and Atlantis have co-operated in this mission.

'As the Atlantis pupils know, I am a wealthy man, and I like to buy things that interest me and make other people happy. And that's why, earlier this week, I have bought the Advanced Marine Academy of the People's Republic of Rockall. 'I have long been providing scholarships to the Academy. The Warden has been doing a fine job, but his premises need some investment, which I will provide.

'So, all you Rockallers will have a nicer school to return to, although I understand Luce wants to offer two of you a scholarship to Atlantis. We'll have to work out the details, but that's for another day. Tonight, enjoy the party!'